"Do you need something?"

He stepped inside and closed the door behind him. "You."

She couldn't have heard that right. All the adrenaline and crackling of her nerves had her brain misfiring. "What did you just say?"

"Nothing."

The mattress dipped from his weight and her body slid into his. "I can't seem to calm my nerves. I feel like I'm six seconds from flying apart."

His palm slipped over her thigh. "It's aftermath."

"Do you always feel like this?"

"Just sometimes." He slid his hand over hers and their fingers entwined. "Your nerve endings are on fire. The danger and fear, the sadness and pain. It's all mixing and getting jammed up inside you."

"How do I get rid of it?"

"Different things work for different people." His thumb rubbed against the back of her hand. Slow, lazy circles that soothed her even as her insides continued to churn.

Bold had worked for her once before. She tried it again. "Any chance kissing does the trick?"

SHELTERED

—

HelenKay Dimon

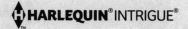

Thank you to my husband, James, for the trip to Oregon.
All that beautiful open space gave me tons of suspense ideas.

Recycling programs
for this product may
not exist in your area.

ISBN-13: 978-0-373-74898-3

Sheltered

Copyright © 2015 by HelenKay Dimon

www.Harlequin.com

Printed in U.S.A.

HelenKay Dimon, an award-winning author, spent twelve years in the most unromantic career ever— divorce lawyer. After dedicating all that effort to helping people terminate relationships, she is thrilled to deal in happy endings and write romance novels for a living. Now her days are filled with gardening, writing, reading and spending time with her family in and around San Diego. Stop by her website, helenkaydimon.com, and say hello.

Books by HelenKay Dimon

HARLEQUIN INTRIGUE

Corcoran Team: Bulletproof Bachelors series

Cornered
Sheltered

Corcoran Team series

Fearless
Ruthless
Relentless
Lawless
Traceless

Mystery Men series

Under the Gun
Guns and the Girl Next Door
Gunning for Trouble
Locked and Loaded
The Big Guns

Visit the Author Profile page at
Harlequin.com for more titles.

CAST OF CHARACTERS

Holt Kingston—The leader of Corcoran's traveling team. He's not a man who trusts easily so an assignment that puts him undercover at a commune seems like the perfect job...until he meets Lindsey Pike. And he doesn't so much meet her as he breaks into her house to prevent her from being kidnapped. He's there to rescue her, but getting her to believe him takes longer. Falling for her? Far too easy.

Lindsey Pike—Lindsey grew up the hard way. She went from being a pawn in her parents' divorce to getting stuck at New Foundations, the cult disguised as a commune nearby. She escaped years ago and now runs an underground group that helps others get out. But when Holt crashes into her life, not only is her carefully crafted cover in danger, but so is her control. What she feels for him threatens everything, and when people start dying, she's not sure where to turn.

Todd Burdock—The sharpshooter who found a home at New Foundations. He's a believer...or maybe just a good soldier. Either way, he does what he's told and he's not convinced Holt is really the handyman he's claiming to be. But knowing he's with Lindsey makes it easier to watch them both. Now he has to decide what to do with them.

Simon Falls—The mysterious man at the center of it all. Simon runs New Foundations and keeps his followers in line. But is he dealing in more than beliefs? The stockpile of weapons at the camp suggests so, but the bigger problem is that his obsession with Lindsey keeps growing.

Frank Carver, Jr.—He earned his job in the sheriff's office the old-fashioned way...by inheriting it from his lawman father. Deputy Carver is green and new. Lindsey thinks he's a little too close to the people at New Foundations. He's not giving any indication who he'll support when the shooting starts, but some family secrets may hold the clue.

Shane Baker—He's Holt's right-hand man and best friend. They've served together and fought together. They made a vow to remain bachelors as the rest of the team paired off, but he sees the way Holt looks at Lindsey. Shane just wishes he could trust her.

Chapter One

For the third night in a row the wind and rain whipped up the Oregon Coast and smacked into the side of Lindsey Pike's small cottage. The temps dipped into lower than normal range for late summer, but that was only part of the reason for keeping her windows closed. The other sat about eleven miles away, up a steep hill and behind a locked gate.

But cool temperature or not, a steady banging put her already zapping nerves further on edge. The rattle came first, then the thud. That would teach her to wait on fixing the shutter in the family room until "sometime next week."

She leaned back into the stack of pillows piled behind her on her bed and reopened her book. After she stared at the same line for what felt like the billionth time, she decided maybe this wasn't the right night for dry research reading. She slipped her legs over the side of the bed and winced when her bare toes hit the chilled hardwood floor.

She made it two steps down the hallway in search of the perfect mindless magazine before she stilled. Something was off. In the air, in the tight space...something.

Up on the balls of her feet, she spun around, thinking to head back to the bedroom and to the gun she kept locked in a safe in her nightstand. Then it hit her. No banging. The wind still howled and the rafters shook now and then. But no more noise.

Torn between possibilities, she stood there. The poor shutter probably finally blew off. That meant hunting it down tomorrow and reattaching it, properly this time. Even as the rationale hung in her mind her unease increased. The slow churning of dread deep in her stomach spun faster. Yeah, she'd lived through paralyzing anxiety before and knew the sensation never led her wrong.

She turned back toward the family room and saw him. It...whatever. Big and looming and shadowed. Without thinking, she took off in a sprint in the opposite direction. Her feet tapped against the floor as she broke for the bedroom. For the gun and the phone. She'd use the lamp as a weapon if she had to. Anything to survive.

Footsteps thundered behind her, louder and

faster. Just as she hit the doorway a hand fell on her shoulder. Fingers clenched against her pajama top and dragged it and her backward. She landed with a thump against a solid mass.

"Listen to me." The deep voice vibrated as he whispered.

"No." She scratched and clawed. "Let go!"

She wound up for the most deafening scream of her life, but it choked off in her throat when his hand landed on her mouth. "Lindsey, stop."

In the haze she didn't recognize the voice. Didn't matter if she did. Forget that he knew her name. This person broke in. She had to get him out or take him down. Those were the only two options. She would not be a victim again.

"Lindsey, it's me." He pulled her in tighter against him, banding an arm around her middle and trapping her legs with one of his.

"Get out," she screamed, but the words got muffled against his palm.

She went with biting. Clamped down hard on the fleshy part of his hand and heard him swear as he jerked back. His arm loosened and she scrambled away. She couldn't get the bedroom door shut, but she could get to that lockbox.

Her heartbeat hammered in her ears as her fingers fumbled with the drawer pull. She'd barely opened it when the attacker knocked her back on the mattress. She flailed, kicking out, trying to land a punch or a hit, or anything that would slow him down or double him over.

Adrenaline pumped through her. Between the race down the hall and the fear pulling at her, she should be exhausted. Instead, energy pulsed through her. She believed she could lift the house, if needed. But first she had to move this guy.

She shoved a knee deep between his legs, but he reached down and caught the shot just in time. With her head shifting on the bed and her body in constant motion, she could barely see. All of her focus went into thinking and moving.

"Lindsey, it's Hank."

His frustration hit her. The words took another second. She maintained her tight grip on his wrist as she looked up. Her gaze went to the broad shoulders and coal-black hair. Those intense dark eyes.

Recognition struck. Right, Hank…something. He was the new handyman, the gofer, whatever his real title, for the New Foundations Retreat. The place she hated most but could not escape.

If he thought letting her make that connection in her mind would make it easier to accept his presence, he was dead wrong. She put anyone affiliated with New Foundations in the "never trust" category. The scruffy rough-and-tumble look would not get him off that list, especially now.

She bucked her hips, trying to knock him off balance. "Get off."

When that failed, panic rolled through her. His weight anchored her to the bed, which left her few options.

"You need to listen," he said in a harsh whisper.

"No." She tried to wiggle her wrist free so she could scratch. If he'd put just a bit of space between their locked bodies, she would knee him hard enough to send him rolling on the floor.

Lightning lit up the room and a crack of thunder came right behind. She remembered childhood tales about the time between them having something to do with the distance you were from the storm. Probably hogwash, but she needed something mindless to block the blinding fear.

He touched her cheek and moved her head until she faced him. He stared down, as if willing her to believe. "Men are coming."

With that her body froze. "What?"

"Some people at New Foundations want to talk to you and I don't think they care if you want to listen."

A new wave of desperation hit her. Maybe he was there to warn her. Maybe he was there to help whoever was coming, if that threat was even true. Didn't matter, because she refused to stick around and see.

Inhaling and trying to calm her breathing, she didn't flinch away from his touch or try to get away. For a few seconds she put all her energy into convincing him. "I have to get out of here."

"I need to keep you safe." He nodded as the grip on her wrists eased. "That's why I'm here."

He broke in and scared the hell out of her. Those facts kept running through her mind and pushing out everything else. "You're one of them."

"Lindsey, no." He shook his head. "I am not here to hurt you."

The calm tone. The orders delivered in an even cadence. She'd experienced it all before, sometimes from well-meaning folks who promised they would help. But those other times weighed on her, had her skepticism snapping. "Why should I believe you?"

"Wish I had a good answer for that, but I don't." He hesitated and then lifted off her, inch by inch, until he balanced on his knees, straddling her. One quick glance down between his legs and he shifted to kneel to the side of her. "I'm only a few steps in front of them."

She'd never been one to get dizzy or faint. Not her style at all, but the oxygen seeped out of her until the room spun and bile raced up her throat. "Let me slip out the back."

"Would never work." He held up his hands as he stepped off the mattress and stood in front of her. "They need to think you're with me."

She jackknifed into a sitting position, ready to make a second grab for the nightstand depending on what he said next. "What?"

"Trust me."

That was never going to happen. Not for him. Not for anyone. Those days were long gone for her. "No way."

She barely got the words out before a crack sounded at the front of the house. A new surge of fear whipped through her.

He glanced behind him as he kept that hand out, gesturing for her to stay down. "Do not move."

From the bed? That wasn't happening either. "I will kill you first."

"And that would be your right if I tried to hurt you, but I won't." The words sounded good, but he started unbuttoning his shirt.

"What are you doing?" But she knew. Knew and would throw every single thing in the room at him, nailed down or not.

He left his blue long-sleeve shirt open over a T-shirt and reached for his belt. A few quick moves and he had the zipper down and the jeans on the floor. "Making it believable."

Her hand inched toward the lamp. The heavy base right to his skull might stop him. "Okay."

But he didn't come at her in his boxer briefs. He bent down and slipped something out of…a gun. With a touch of a finger to his lips he turned toward the doorway.

"Who's there?" His deep voice echoed down the hall.

She had no idea what was happening. Shadows moved outside her window. She assumed branches, but she didn't know. Everything blended together and morphed until the walls pounded in on her.

He kicked off his shoes and stepped into the hallway. The floorboards creaked under his weight.

She thought about diving out the window but had no idea what lurked out there. Forcing her mind to focus, she grabbed for the nightstand drawer. Punched in the lock code and had the gun loaded and in her hand as she crept out behind Hank.

"I am not going to let you touch my girlfriend." He kept his back against the wall as he slid farther down the hall toward the family room. "Leave now and this ends fine."

My girlfriend? Her mind stuck there and

refused to unstick. The most she could do was stand up and get to the bedroom doorway.

She stopped in time to see the collision. Hank took one more step and a body smashed into him. She aimed her gun, but only darkness greeted her. The two men were locked in battle, rolling like a ball across her floor. She heard grunts and saw arms rise and fall. One back thumped against the hallway wall, then another.

Lightning flashed and she saw blond hair and a dark jacket. She didn't recognize the intruder. Only Hank. She could make him out as he landed punch after punch against the blond's jaw.

Thunder boomed and then an eerie quiet fell over the back of the house. The men tumbled as they slipped out of sight. Something fell to the floor with a crash, but the usual buzz of the lights and hum of the refrigerator had stopped. She reached out and flicked the switch by her head, but nothing happened. Either the storm knocked out the power or a group of men outside her home did. She hated both options.

Gripping the gun, she stepped into the hall and tried to make out one figure from the other. She didn't know Hank and didn't owe him anything, but he could have dragged her outside and handed her to the blond. He hadn't, and the confusion from that kept her from shooting him now.

But she could see shapes. Hank had the blond on the floor. Hank's legs pinned the guy, and an arm hooked around his neck. Looked to her as though her make-believe boyfriend had this one won. Nothing about that realization had her relaxing.

The scuffle continued. The blond's heels smacked against the floor. The battle seemed to be dying down until another figure stepped into the far end of the hall opposite her. Her insides chilled and her body shook hard enough for her teeth to rattle. She couldn't make out his face but got the impression he was staring at her. Waiting.

One swing of his arm and he knocked Hank's head into the wall. She aimed, ready to fire at anyone who came toward her. But the newest man reached down and dragged the blond to his feet. Then they were gone.

She stood there, unable to think. Unable to breathe.

"Lindsey?" Hank stumbled to his feet as he scooped his gun off the floor. "You okay?"

His voice snapped her out of her stupor. She reached inside her bedroom and ripped the emergency flashlight out of the socket, then grabbed the second one she kept just inside the bathroom door.

She fumbled to hold them both in one hand and aimed them in Hank's direction. He blinked as he rubbed one hand over the back of his head. The other one, the one with the weapon, dropped to his side.

His gaze traveled over her, and then he frowned. "Where did you get a gun?"

Not exactly the response she'd expected, but until he asked she forgot she held it. "It's mine."

"Maybe you could lower it."

She wanted to ask if he was okay. After all, unless he'd put on some great show, he'd just saved her from two intruders storming in and taking her away. But that wasn't where her mind went. "Who are you?"

At first she didn't think he heard her. He walked through the small house. Checked the front door. Looked outside.

He finally turned back to her. "You should think of me as Hank Fletcher. A handyman who blew into town looking for work. We met, started dating and now I'm at your house most nights."

Wrong answer, and that was before she got to the boyfriend thing. She ignored that part completely. "But that's not who you are."

"No."

At least he didn't lie or try to shrug her off. But she still wanted an answer. "Tell me or the gun stays up."

He leaned against the armrest of her couch. "Holt Kingston, undercover with the Corcoran Team, and right now the best hope you have of not being dragged up to the compound and questioned."

She had no idea what any of that meant but grabbed on to the "undercover" part and hoped that stood for police or law enforcement. Really, anyone with a gun and some authority who could help.

Going further, the idea of trusting him even the slightest bit brought her common sense to a screeching halt. But as much as it grated, there was something about him. It had been that way from the beginning. She'd seen him in town and driving the New Foundations truck and she couldn't stop watching. She chalked the reaction up to being cautious, but what she was thinking of doing right now, letting him in if only an inch, struck her as reckless.

Even now, standing there in his underwear, with this massive chest and...well, everything looked pretty big. Still, the fear that had gripped her body and held it to that spot in the hall eased away. Tension buzzed through the room, but the panic had subsided.

Ignoring the warning bells dinging in her head, she verbally reached out. "So, you know New Foundations is a cult."

"Oh, Lindsey." He shook his head. "It's worse than that. So much more dangerous and threatening."

At least he understood that much about the place that starred in her nightmares. That was more than her father ever understood. "Okay, then."

His shoulders dropped a little, as if the tension stiffening them had ratcheted down. "So, we're good?"

No way was she going that far. Not yet. Probably not ever. "Let's just say I'm willing to hear you out."

"That's all I'm asking."

She let the hand with the gun drop to her side but didn't let go. "Talk fast."

Chapter Two

Holt felt the tension ease from his shoulders the second she dropped the gun. The close call would teach him to break protocol. He'd overheard two New Foundations bruisers talking about grabbing Lindsey and snapped into action. Gone to her house and the rest was a combination of pure luck and timing.

Not that he usually dropped cover. He rescued for a living. That was what the Corcoran Team did. Worked undercover in off-the-books operations, preventing kidnappings before they happened and when called in too late, being the first to rush in and get victims out. Hired by governments and corporations, they performed work others couldn't.

His three-man team moved constantly but reported back to the main office in Annapolis. Connor Bowen owned the company and ran the show, including the four agents who worked out of Maryland. Holt only had to check in with one person—Connor—and the boss would not like how this assignment had spun out.

Holt could hardly admit getting his head turned by a pretty woman. And Lindsey Pike definitely qualified as that. She possessed a girl-next-door prettiness. The shiny brown hair with streaks of blond. The big green eyes. The confident way she moved around the town of Justice, Oregon, the most ill-named town ever.

She'd intrigued him from day one, and hearing she was in trouble tonight got him moving.

Now he figured he had about ten seconds to convince her that he was one of the good guys or see her whip out that gun again. Actually, from the frown, maybe more like five.

"Tell me exactly why you're here." Her expression didn't change. Those lips stayed in a flat line as a sort of grim determination moved over her.

No shock. No panic. That told him she knew exactly how dangerous the folks at New Foundations were. Maybe she'd expected them to hunt her down. Maybe she'd been poking at them. Either way, she appeared to possess the type of intel he needed.

In cases like this, with the adrenaline still pumping, the simple truth tended to work, so he went with it. "There were orders to bring you in."

"From?"

He had a feeling the call came from high up, but he couldn't pinpoint it yet. "I don't know."

If possible, her frown deepened. "Of course you do. Who told you to come after me?"

That explained it. She still viewed him as attacker, not rescuer. "No one. I overheard men talking at the compound and got here first to warn you."

"Compound." She scoffed. "The place almost sounds nice when you say it that way."

Not what he'd seen. Sure, on the surface, everything ticked along fine. The camp operated as a retreat. Cabins lined up in a serene wooded area. Communal gardens and shared meals in a dining hall. Staff had the option of living in less private bunkhouses a few hundred feet from the main area, behind the yoga studio.

It all seemed peaceful, the perfect place for people who were tired of being plugged in and those sick of government regulations or city life. But on the inside something festered. Groups of men would leave for hours at a time. The gun range had a steady stream of customers. So did the makeshift village built on the back of the property. The one where people practiced drills storming houses and learning how to fight off attacks.

But none of that worried Holt like the sheer

amount of firepower he'd seen brought onto the property. He recognized the crates and couldn't come up with a single reason a retreat that featured yoga would also have grenade launchers.

Corcoran had been sent in after information leaked. But finding former members proved difficult. People went there and stayed, which had government officials thinking cult. That was what Holt had expected on this assignment, but now he knew better. New Foundations had the makings of a homegrown militia.

He stepped carefully with Lindsey now, hoping he'd finally found a thread he could pull to bring the place down. "Apparently you ticked off someone at the retreat."

"You have no idea."

But he wanted to know. With her, he guessed the direct question might not get the job done, so he verbally walked around it, hoping to land on the information he needed. "Were you a member?"

She tightened her grip on the gun. "For now, I think I'll ask the questions."

The woman played this well. He admired her refusal to get sucked in. "Why do you think I'll agree to that?"

"You are in my house. You dragged me out of bed, stripped down and—"

"Fine." Round One to Lindsey. "Go ahead."

Using the hand with the gun, she motioned for him to sit down on the couch. "What's the Corcoran Team?"

He settled for leaning against the armrest because he had a feeling he needed to be up and ready to fight with this woman. "Can't tell you that."

She stood right in front of him, close but not close enough for him to grab the gun or get a jump on her. If he didn't know better, he'd say she'd been trained. And if he was right that she'd spent some time at the retreat and lived to talk about it, her survival instincts might rival his own.

"Are you with the government?"

"With?" He knew what she was asking but didn't know if she knew.

"An FBI agent or something."

The out waited right there and he took it. "Or something."

She sighed at him. Threw out one of those long-suffering exhales that women did so well when men ticked them off. "I feel like we're going backward here."

"We'll get to all that, but first we're going to contact the police." He should have made the call as soon as the attackers left.

"No." That was all she said. A curt denial.

People generally didn't question his orders.

Probably had something to do with his size and no-room-for-debate scowl. His sister said he'd inherited the look and demeanor from their dad. Holt knew that wasn't exactly a compliment.

"Excuse me?" He kept his voice deadly soft in an attempt to telegraph his mood to her.

Her eyebrow lifted. "Oh, I'm thinking you heard me."

This woman didn't scare easily. He had to admit he found that, along with everything else about her, smoking hot. The not-backing-down thing totally worked for him.

Not that he had time for anything but work, which led him right back to his point. "We need to file a report."

"We know who attacked. You just confirmed it. You came here to stop it…I guess."

Her refusal to get that point had his temper spiking, but he didn't let it show. He never let it show. He didn't need the West Point education and years in the army after to teach him how to remain calm. For him, playing this game amounted to common sense and he could pull off outward disinterest even while his insides churned. "The people at New Foundations can't know I'm onto them."

"Why?" Her tone now rang with interest, as if she were trying to fit the pieces together in her head.

"I'm working undercover, which means you can't say anything." He'd already blown that one, but since she hadn't shot in him in the head he believed he'd made the right call.

"Who would I tell?"

That wasn't exactly his point. "I have no idea."

She hesitated while her gaze toured his face. "Let's talk about the undercover thing for a bit."

Yeah, enough sharing. "After we call the police."

She shook her head. Looked even more determined to shut down his plan. "The police around here protect the people who run New Foundations. They have some sort of relationship that keeps the camp in business."

Holt got that. There would need to be some sort of quid pro quo for the retreat to operate in such an information vacuum. At least he hoped so. "I'm counting on that."

Her stance eased and some of the tension tightening her shoulders disappeared. "You lost me."

A quick once-over glance told him some of her fear had subsided. The glance also tugged on his concentration. Her pajamas, the lack of a bra...he noticed it all.

He forced his mind back to the conversation and off her body and that face...man, she was killing him. "We have one hope of keeping you safe."

"What's that?"

"Me."

She treated him to a second sigh, this one longer than the first. She also put her gun down on the table at the end of the couch. "I knew you were going to say that."

No need to spook her, so he didn't make a move or even look at the gun, even though it sat just inches from his thigh. "If they think we're dating, I become more helpful."

"How?" The skepticism in her voice slammed into him.

He gritted his teeth as he tried to ignore the attitude. "You stay protected."

"Why wouldn't they just grab me?"

A fine question, which led him to one of his own. "Why do they want to?"

"Don't know." She folded her arms across her midsection. "Ask them."

"Are you always this difficult?" She was almost as prickly as he was when it came to holding back information. He admired the skill even as it blocked him from getting the intel he needed.

"Yes."

The honesty was pretty hot, too. Still, Holt knew his plan provided the right answer. "We call the police. We file a report. The report gets back to the New Foundations folks and my cover holds. With all that in place, it becomes that much harder for them to grab you."

She shrugged. "Or I could leave town."

A good plan. The smart one. For some reason not one he liked very much. "That's the better option, but I was betting you'd say no if I suggested it."

"Why?"

"In addition to the fact that you seem to question everything I say?"

The corner of her mouth lifted in what looked like an almost-smile. "I'm tempted to deny that, but I fear it would prove your point."

Since he felt as though he actually won that round, he answered the original question. "The people I'm protecting usually refuse to leave their homes, family, friends…you get the picture."

He'd heard the refrain so many times that he was starting to believe Connor's argument that people valued family and home above all else. Not one to stick around in one place for very long, Holt didn't really get it.

He had people in his life he'd die for and a job he loved, but the whole craving a home thing never registered with him. Maybe it stemmed from having a father more dedicated to the army than his kids.

Maybe it was what happened when the person you trusted most left you to die on an abandoned stretch of dirt road in Afghanistan. Holt suspected that didn't help, but it didn't really matter how he got to the emotional freeze-out, because that was his reality and he didn't see it changing.

"You do this a lot?" she asked.

"Rescue? Yeah, it's all I do." All he knew.

The final bit of tension zapping around the room ceased. "So you can actually shoot that thing?"

He followed her gaze to his gun. The one she could see. "Yes, ma'am."

"You're not a handyman."

It was his turn to shrug. "I'm handy."

"Oh, really?"

"I've got skills." He needed to pull back. Knew it but didn't.

Her expression changed then. "Are you flirting with me?"

So tempting. "That would be bad form, since two guys just tried to kick my butt." He needed to stay on his feet and aware, though he could understand why she asked. His gaze kept wandering. So did his thoughts.

Not good at all.

"I don't understand any of what's going on tonight. I've seen you around town. I stay away from the camp and never say anything about what goes on there." She broke away and walked toward the kitchen, then paced back.

She walked with her movements jerky for the first time. Frustration pulsed off her.

Yeah, he needed this intel. He felt for her, but she talked about knowing what happened in the camp. Didn't say she "heard" tales. No, she had personal knowledge. He'd bet on it. "You're saying you don't know what you did to upset the New Foundations people?"

"Of course I do."

Round and round they went. She gave new meaning to the term *pulling teeth*. "And?"

"My entire life is dedicated to ruining that place."

Bingo. "Well, then…"

She pointed in the general direction of the front door. "They don't know that."

"Clearly they do." And she had him curious. Her hatred sounded personal. That could mean she once lived there. She might know about former members. People his team needed to interview.

"You are not the only one working undercover. For me, it's more like working underground." She went back to pacing. "And up until tonight no one ever bothered me. I live just far enough away, keep my name out of the papers and protests. I drive miles outside of my way just so I can avoid driving near the entrance."

When he couldn't take the quiet tap of her bare feet against the hardwood one more second, he stepped in front of her. "Maybe someone recognized you."

He needed more details but decided not to press because whatever the reason, she'd landed on someone's radar screen. That meant the life she knew and protected was over.

Her head snapped up. "It could be worse than that."

"How?"

Tension tightened her features again. "Someone up there must have figured out who I really am."

Chapter Three

Simon Falls leaned back in his desk chair. The only desk chair on the property. Everyone else preferred mats and cushy chairs. He wanted a stiff-backed seat that put him face-to-face with the monitors on the wall and in front of him. Security feeds, including two rotating video shots of places in town.

Now was not the time to descend into touchy-feely madness. He'd leave the talk about privacy and personal space to the workshop leaders. No one paid him to hold hands. His job came down to one simple idea: protect the camp at any cost. A task that would be easier if everyone did their job, which brought his mind back to this meeting.

He tapped his pen against the desk blotter as he stared at the two men he depended on to handle trouble. This time they'd failed him. He'd handed them one assignment—grab the girl and bring her back unharmed.

They'd run into trouble and had all sorts of excuses. Only one interested Simon.

"What man?" When neither underling answered him, Simon tried again. "At the house. Give me the identity."

"It was Hank Fletcher, one of the newer guys on our staff." Todd Burdock, the best shot in the camp, gave his assessment while standing at attention.

Simon turned the information over in his mind. "You're saying Hank is dating Lindsey Pike."

Todd frowned as if he were choosing his words carefully. "I'm saying he was sleeping over."

Grant Whiddle nodded. "No question they're together."

None of that information matched the surveillance. Simon watched Lindsey. Had watched her for months once the whispers started and the background investigation ran him into a wall. "Since when?"

Todd shook his hand. "I don't know."

Not a sufficient answer, and the man should know that. Simon did not countenance failure. Not here. Not on his watch. "Find out."

"We can call him in," Grant suggested.

Simon knew that was the exact wrong answer.

That was the reason he ran camp security and the two in front of him didn't.

"Hank is not to know we were behind tonight's incident." That would make tracking impossible, and now Simon had a new person to track. "No, this needs to be handled differently. Who does Hank know at the compound?"

"No one. He sticks to himself," Todd said without giving eye contact. Then again, he never did.

But Hank was the issue here. A loner. No surprise there. They littered the camp. Disillusioned men who needed a purpose filled the beds and the coffers. They came with what little they owned and handed it over in exchange for a promise.

Simon remembered tagging Hank as one of those types during his interview. Dishonorably discharged for firing when any sane person would fire. He had potential plus a gift for shooting. And he might still work out, but that didn't mean the Lindsey Pike connection could be ignored.

"He lives at the bunkhouse." Simon knew because he'd assigned Hank the space. "Is this his first night away from the compound since arriving?"

Grant gave Todd a quick look before speaking. "No."

That didn't quite match up with Simon's view of the man or with what Simon saw on the monitors day after day. Hank did his job, never wavered, rarely asked questions. But everyone had an agenda, and Simon would find Hank's.

"We need a closer watch on him. I want every minute accounted for, including those with Lindsey." Especially those with Lindsey.

"So we're not bringing her up to camp now?" Grant asked.

The question screeched across Simon's nerves. So stupid. That was the problem with hired guns. They didn't always come with brains. "You can't very well try to drag her out of her house two nights in a row. She'll be expecting you."

Grant shook his head. "But we'll be expecting Hank this time. We can take another guy and—"

Enough. "The original mission is on hold until we know more about Hank." Simon dismissed them by returning to watch his monitors.

Todd cleared his voice. "She is potentially dangerous, sir."

"She is." Simon stared at the men again. "So am I. You would both be wise to remember that."

THE COUNTY SHERIFF'S office proved less helpful than Lindsey had expected. She didn't want to file a report or even involve law enforcement. That opened the door into an investigation, which meant someone could stumble over pieces of her past. Pieces she'd kept hidden for years.

"Vagrants." Deputy Carver made that announcement after his walk-through of her house.

The guy had been on the job for about eight months. He'd earned it the old-fashioned way, by taking over when his father had a heart attack. The elder Frank Carver went into the hospital and then rehab and now waited out his disability leave at home as he worked to get his strength back.

The younger Frank Carver stepped in. Never mind he was green and over his head, he'd grown up in this town. Knew everyone by name.

What Frank Carver, Jr., with his red hair and cheeks stained red the way they did anytime he talked with anyone, lacked in experience, he made up for in sheer shooting ability and endurance. He'd simply been tagging along after his father long enough to be considered a fixture. Combine that with the town's love and loyalty to his father, and the kid wasn't going anywhere.

He wasn't doing anything to help her either. She fought the urge to say "I told you so" to Holt. Settled for mouthing it instead.

The deputy had done exactly what she'd predicted—nothing. No forensics. No photos. He just walked around with Holt at his heels.

"No other answer, really." Deputy Carver

took a closer look at the doorjamb. Studied it. Even got up on his tiptoes since the thick-soled shoes only put him at five nine, and that was just barely. "You said they weren't kids."

Holt stood there, studying whatever Deputy Carver studied and shaking his head. "These were grown men."

"Good thing you were here, then, Mr. Fletcher." Deputy Carver shot Holt a man-to-man look.

"You can call me Hank."

She was impressed Holt refrained from rolling his eyes. At six-foot-something, he towered over the kid. Also looked as if he could break the deputy in half. The contrast in their sizes and confidence, styles and stance could not have been more pronounced. At twenty-four, Frank Jr. had to be a decade or so younger than Holt, but the difference in maturity shone through.

Not that she was looking…but she couldn't really stop looking. Recognizing Holt standing in her house had shaken her. He didn't belong there. She'd locked the doors, performed her nightly safety check. But that wasn't what had her rattled to the point where her teeth still chattered.

No, she'd been thinking about him. A lot, every day, at odd times. Ever since she'd seen him in town weeks before, he'd played a role in her dreams. The quiet stranger who walked into town, didn't ask questions and swept her right into the bed. Pure fantasy wrapped in a tall, dark and dangerous package. The broad shoulders and trim waist, the coal-black hair and the hint in his features of Asian ancestry.

She blamed the dark eyes and brooding look. That was why she stared. She'd see him around town and she'd watch, her gaze following him, then skipping away when he'd look back. The whole thing made her feel like a naughty teen, but it had been so long since she'd felt anything for a man that she welcomed the sensation.

"I'd hate to think what could have happened," Deputy Carver said, droning on.

Holt waved the younger man off. "But it didn't, so we're good."

She tried to ignore the deputy's attempts at male bonding and the way both men talked around her, as if she weren't even in the room.

But this was her house. Her life. "For the record, I can use a gun."

"Of course." The deputy didn't even spare her a glance before talking to Holt again. "I don't think I've seen you around. Are you new in town?"

"I work odd jobs at New Foundations."

Lindsey couldn't figure out if this amounted to the deputy's attempt to question Holt or if the younger man was so enamored that the staring reflected some sort of weird hero worship. Either way, it was getting late and she needed to clean up and get to bed.

"Good work. Good people up there." Frank Jr. tucked the small pad of paper back into his pocket without ever taking a note.

"Yeah, right." Not that anyone asked her, but she threw the words out there anyway. When Holt smiled, she figured he at least got her point about being ignored.

"And you're with Ms. Pike." The comment came out of the blue.

Holt didn't show any outward reaction. She had to bite back a groan.

Here we go. "Are you asking about my love life?" She really wanted to know.

"Of course not." The deputy looked at her for the first time. A short look. Long enough to frown, but that was about it. "Just making an observation."

"We're together." Holt inched closer to her.

She hadn't actually noticed him moving, but one second he stood by the door and the next he stood beside her. She concentrated for a second, tried to block out the whoosh of blood through her ears and the comforting feel of his hand low on her back. Long fingers. A warm palm.

She almost choked, and not from fear. No, this churning felt much more like excitement.

"We'll let you know if we find anything, but I'm sure this was a once and done. Probably someone looking for drugs or money for drugs." The deputy took out his car keys. He hadn't run down the porch steps but looked two seconds away from taking off.

Holt's questions stopped him. "Is there a big drug problem around here?"

"Isn't there everywhere?" Frank Jr. asked as he glanced over his shoulder at them.

"Then it's good I'm living here now. With Lindsey." Holt's voice rang out.

He didn't yell, but he might as well have. It felt as if even the breeze stopped blowing. He sure had her attention.

The deputy turned the full way around and faced them. Kept his focus on Holt as an atta-boy grin crept across his lips. "Is that right?"

She had the opposite reaction. Shock rolled over her. Pretending to be her boyfriend was one thing, and she hadn't even agreed to that yet. Being her live-in sounded much bigger. To the people in town and everyone at the camp, it would be bigger. But she guessed that was the point.

She hadn't worked it all out in her head when Holt's fingers tightened against her back. Ready or not, it seemed he wanted her support. She coughed it up. "Uh, yeah."

The deputy just stared. Stood on the bottom step and looked them both up and down, never bothering to close his mouth or hide his delight at being the first to dig up this small-town gossip. "Then you have even less reason for worry."

"That's how I look at it." Holt nodded in what came off as a dismissal.

The deputy must have gotten the hint, because he walked the rest of the way down the steps and to his car. Didn't say anything about the attack in the house or give her any warning or advice. It was as if Holt had spoken and that resolved everything.

While she liked not having to answer questions, the way the whole scene rolled out had her feeling twitchy. Someone broke into *her* house and went after *her*, and only Holt mattered to the deputy.

She knew who—New Foundations—and why, but she doubted the deputy did. She'd done everything to keep her past and true identity hidden. Revealing it now out of frustration was not the right answer, so she let the whole thing drop.

Well, not all of it. There was still the small bit of gloating she planned to do. "That was a waste of time. I'll refrain from saying 'told you so' a few hundred times."

Holt took one step down. The move put them close to eye-to-eye. "Again, the point of that exercise was to send a message. We accomplished that."

"You want people to think we're not looking at New Foundations as the culprit." She got it. The more she thought about the long term, the more she appreciated Holt stepping in with a rational head.

She wasn't the type to run on emotions, but facing down men with a gun threw off her emotional balance. She still fought to regain a sense of normalcy...or what passed for normalcy for her.

"That and to establish me as the guy they have to get through before they can touch you," Holt said.

That part didn't quite fit together in her head. "Speaking of which—"

Holt leaned against the beam holding up this side of the porch. "When they think I live here it becomes less likely they come back."

"You think they'll just leave me alone?"

"No."

Not exactly the answer she'd expected. The guy could use a lesson or two in tact. "That's not very comforting."

"I was going for honest."

And she had to appreciate that. She'd spent a lot of her life trying to ferret out emotions and counteract the games people played. Holt appeared to be a straight shooter. She knew on one level she should love that, but when it came to being dragged out of her own house, she needed a little reassurance.

She also needed to set some ground rules.

"Then, honestly, you should know you're not living here." The last thing she needed was a walking, talking fantasy sleeping on her couch. Dreaming about him already messed with her sleep. Having him nearby, hearing him, smelling him, being able to look at him all the time, might just break her control.

Instead of commenting on her point, Holt crossed his arms over that impressive chest. "You danced around it before. Now tell me exactly why they want you. While you're at it, you can finally tell me what you meant an hour ago with that talk about your identity. Maybe start with how many you have."

Yeah, she could play this game, too. He stood on her turf. That should count for something. As far as she was concerned, he should go first. "Only if you tell me exactly what you're really doing here and why. You can also throw in who sent you. Maybe give me a list of what you've found out so far."

Standing there in the quiet he didn't say touché, but she sensed it.

"Impressive." He smiled. "I think we're at an impasse."

The twinkle in his dark eyes and that dimple in his cheek...oh, so tempting. She had to marshal all her resources to push back and fight off the energy zipping around inside her. "That still doesn't get you a bed for the night."

"I'll take the couch."

This guy had a ready response for everything. "Hank...Holt..." She actually didn't know which was right, let alone who he really was and if he could be trusted. Her instincts told her yes, but even letting him plant the seed about being in a relationship with her amounted to a big risk. "Okay, I give up. What do I call you?"

"In public, Hank. If it makes it easier and helps you remember not to slip up, always call me that."

She preferred Holt. The name fit him. It felt big and secure and special. Not that she could let him know any of that. "I don't know you."

He winked at her. "Right back at ya."

Maybe it was the voice, all rough and husky. Maybe it was the fact he could have hurt her a dozen times, dragged her right up to the compound or let the two goons who broke into her house do it. For whatever reason, a sense of calm washed over her when he came around.

She wished she knew why. "Why should I trust you?"

"You don't have a choice."

Wrong. That was the one thing—possibly the only helpful thing—she'd learned from her father. "People always have a choice."

Holt shrugged. "Fine. Leave town until it's safe."

He gave her the out and she should have grabbed it. The words sat right there on her tongue. She could leave, take a few days away and get her bearings. But the idea of leaving him, of running, made her stomach fall. "When will that be?"

"I don't know."

The guy did do honesty well. It didn't always serve his case, yet he stuck with it. She liked that about him. That and those shoulders…and the face…and the hair that looked so soft. "I have work to do."

"Which is what exactly?"

She couldn't exactly say: rescuing people from the camp. That would open a whole new line of questioning, and she was not ready to go there with him. Or with anyone. "We're spinning in circles."

His arms dropped to his sides and he moved in closer. "Look, I get that you're afraid and wary and don't know me. Up until a few hours ago

I only knew you as the woman in town who looked so hot in dark jeans."

Wait... "What?"

He just kept talking. "Now I know you're messed up in New Foundations, which is a crappy thing to be. Some of the people up there are dangerous, possibly delusional."

They were all those things and more. She knew because she'd lived there, fought them. Escaped and hadn't stopped emotionally running since. "I need to stop them."

"You need to stay away and let me take care of them." His eyebrow lifted. "You just have to trust me."

She wanted to believe. She'd been in this battle so long exhaustion had crept into her bones. The idea of turning over the reins and walking away sounded like sweet relief. But she knew things that he didn't, and not seeing this through would slowly pick away at her.

No, she needed to bring down New Foundations on her own. Every cabin. Every workshop. Send every person home.

If only Holt didn't look so sincere. His laser-like gaze never slipped. He watched her until she started to squirm in her skin. She knew what he wanted and she couldn't give it to him. "You're asking a lot."

"I know."

His ready acceptance chipped away at her defenses, just as so much of him did. "You seem to take for granted I'll look at that face and those shoulders and fall in line."

He cleared his throat. "You like my shoulders?"

He stood very close now. Right there until only a few feet separated their bodies. His ego just might kill her.

Time to bring him back down to earth. "You're missing the point."

"I am here to assess what's happening at the compound, determine the danger level and, if necessary, get people out before things blow up. Literally."

That sounded so promising. She'd been stymied by her limited resources and inability to safely infiltrate the fence surrounding the place. To divulge everything to him might help her case against the camp, but it would put her identity at risk. The constant balancing act got old.

Still, if he really could help, really was willing to step in, she couldn't ignore that offer. "But you're not FBI."

He shook his head. "Not FBI or ATF."

"I want to believe you're one of the good guys." But that left a lot of other possibilities, both legitimate and not.

He held up three fingers. "Give me three days to prove it to you."

That icy reserve melted inside her. She felt that resistance give way and her need to say yes overwhelm her. With him she might make progress. He wasn't promising the impossible. He was offering protection, and right now it looked as if she needed it. Maybe together they could work through what the people at the camp knew and what they wanted.

At least that was her assessment. She still needed to know his. "And during those three days?"

His gaze bounced up and down her body, heating a trail as it went. "You get a pretend boyfriend with good shoulders."

He'd hit upon the one thing she could no longer resist. "Deal."

Chapter Four

For the first time since throwing in with the Corcoran Team, Holt seriously considered not showing up at the prearranged time for a meeting the next morning. This one took place two towns over. He'd lost his tail easily and doubled back, circled around. Now he stood in the storage room of a hardware store with his men, waiting for them to snap out of their joint stupor.

He'd known the crap storm he'd wade into the second he opened his mouth and filled them in on what had happened last night, including the part where he camped out on Lindsey's couch. He stuck to the facts and rapid-fired his way through them in his oral report.

Fallout time.

"You did what?" Shane Baker, Holt's best friend and the man he trusted most in the world, looked as if he couldn't fight off his smile.

The openmouthed staring had given way to

smirks, which meant Holt needed a new topic of conversation. "Let's move on."

"When do we get to give you a hard time for picking a woman over the job?"

Holt reassessed his decision to lay out all the facts. He should have skipped right over the Lindsey piece, but Shane was about to walk into town playing the role of an old military buddy. For the fake romantic relationship with Lindsey to work, Shane needed to play along. That meant coming clean...unfortunately.

"Never," Holt said, wondering how to regain control of the conversation. Taking on two of them made it tough.

The snorting sound came the second before Shane's response. "Wrong answer."

Cameron Roth, the team's flying expert, shook his head. "Sorry, man. It's happening."

Holt thought he'd at least have an ally in Cam. The guy had run into a similar situation with a woman and a mess followed by a rescue three months before. "Should we talk about you and Julia and how you had us all racing through an abandoned shipyard to save you?"

"Huh." Cam made a face. "That's not how I remember it."

Shane held up a hand. "Wait, are you comparing your situation with Lindsey to Cam's sad lovesick whining over Julia?"

Cam shook his head again. "I don't remember that either."

"Oh, please." Shane took a seat on a stack of boxes balanced against a wall. "You fell in love and got stupid."

Holt felt a punch of relief when Shane and Cam went after each other and jumped over him. Comparing his relationship with Lindsey to the one shared by Cam and Julia, a couple on the verge of getting engaged, did not amount to a good strategy. But he'd dodged that disaster.

Now he needed his men back on track, and fast. "We're on limited time here."

Fully engaged now, Shane crossed one ankle over the other and leaned in. "Then let's get back to your cover."

Not exactly where Holt wanted to take the next round of conversation. "What about it? It's intact."

"Do we know that or are you going to get called in to see the boss at the camp and get shot?" Cam asked.

"The thing with Lindsey makes me more interesting to management." Being followed ever since he left Lindsey's house clued Holt in. He'd gone from being one of the many faceless men roaming around the campground handling odd jobs to a person they watched.

Not that the person following him could be

called an expert. No, the guy closed in too fast and showed too much interest. He also managed to pick a vehicle Holt recognized as regularly being parked in Simon Falls's private garage. Not a New Foundations company vehicle but one Holt had already staked out during his late-night recon on the property.

Shane frowned. "Which is the problem, since the point was to blend."

"This is better." Every minute Holt became more convinced and he'd get Connor on board in the next hour or so.

Lindsey's intel placed a target—whatever it was, and he'd get that out of her soon enough—on her forehead. That put Holt in the middle, and if he was going to sit there he might as well use the position.

The system worked like a circle. He wanted the information Lindsey possessed, and now someone at New Foundations would want to know what he knew. Either that or eliminate him, and Holt had no intention of letting that option happen.

Shane's frown deepened with each question. "How can the impromptu plan you're using now be better than the one we worked out for a week, taking all contingencies into account?"

All contingencies except Lindsey. Nothing

prepared Holt for her, but he didn't volunteer that piece of information.

"Because under his new plan he gets to sleep at Lindsey's house." Cam twisted the top off the water bottle in his hand. "She is the prize here."

"It's not like that." And Holt would work very hard to keep it that way. He was not a dating guy and he never fooled around on a job.

Cam saluted him with the water bottle. "Yet."

The man-to-man look from Cam made Holt worry they'd never stay on task, so he looked to Shane for help. "I need you on this."

"What's the 'this' you're talking about?"

"Watching over Lindsey when I can't." Holt had to keep up the job at the camp. That meant leaving her without protection. Enter Hank Fletcher's old friend in town for a few weeks.

The cover gave Shane an excuse to hang around. Cam could continue to fly tourists around on the helicopter while really conducting aerial searches of the campground and surrounding areas.

"Does she know she's about to get a second roommate?" Shane asked.

Since she barely wanted one man in the house, Holt hadn't exactly jumped at offering details between coffee and cereal at the kitchen sink this morning. "No."

"Can I be there when she finds out you plan

to spring me on her?" Shane's smile could only be described as annoying.

Holt hid a wince. "Go away."

"Make up your mind." Shane dragged out the sing-songy voice. "You want me to stay. You want me to go."

"To the public we were in the military together. Met there, served and remained friends through everything." Connor and Joel had set up the cover. "Now you're out and looking for a place to land, but you were there when I shot the locals in Afghanistan. You think I got a raw deal."

New Foundations sought out disgruntled men with skills. That meant Holt had needed a story that fit the type. And since he had a horror story of his own in his past, it wasn't all that hard to call up those feelings of frustration.

The difference was he didn't blame the army for what had happened to him. In real life, he'd been the one left to die by someone he trusted. In his cover story, he did the killing. He hated both end results, but he'd lived with the realities of one of them for years now.

"You said that's the story to the public. Interesting word choice." Cam and Shane started talking at the same time, but Cam rushed to finish first. "Are you saying you're going to tell Lindsey who I really am?"

Didn't matter who spoke up, because the answer didn't change. "She already knows my real name and about Corcoran."

"How did that happen again?" Cam asked.

And that brought them right back to where the conversation had started. Instead of staying on the ride, Holt jumped off and started doing what he did best—issuing orders.

He looked at Cam. "You keep up the flights. Take photos. Send them back to Joel and Connor and see if they can make sense of what you're seeing."

Joel Kidd took the lead on Corcoran's tech needs. He could make sense out of nonsense better than anyone Holt knew. And Connor was just about the most competent man on the planet. Holt trusted them to help all the way from Maryland.

"And what about Lindsey?"

"What are you talking about?" But Holt got Cam's point. Connor led Corcoran by a few simple rules to get the job done—collect all the information you can before going in, trust your team and know that Connor would come behind you and clean up the mess.

"The Maryland office, Joel in particular, needs to rip her life apart. Investigate her." Shane slipped into protocol-speak. When no one said anything, he looked around the closed-in room. "What, am I wrong?"

Cam shook his head. "He isn't."

Not in the mood for an argument, Holt conceded. He'd planned to conduct some research into Lindsey and her past. He'd just hoped to do it on a limited basis, without the entire Corcoran Team watching. Apparently that was not going to happen. "Fine."

"She's going to love it when she finds out we're digging into her past," Shane said.

Holt knew the easy answer for that. "We're not going to tell her."

"Yeah, I've found that's not the best strategy with women. You think it'll be fine, but it never works out that way." Cam clapped a hand against Holt's shoulder. "But you keep living in your fantasy world and thinking you control this thing with her."

"I can." Holt was impressed with how strong his voice sounded.

Cam shook his head. "I almost feel bad for you."

LINDSEY SLIPPED OUT onto her porch later that evening. The sun had started to set and a stray cool breeze kicked up. Summers this close to the water and tucked into the base of the woods meant still needing a sweater some nights.

For as long as she could remember, she'd loved sitting outside, watching the sun go down. After years of living at the campground and adhering to all the rules, she enjoyed her freedom. No early morning rising for chores and gun practice. No lectures.

But tonight the air carried a chill and it cut right through her. She'd spent the day making contingency plans if she had to move out without notice. She'd contacted the former New Foundations members she helped place in alternative living situations and gone over the go codes and emergency evacuation drills.

Somewhere in there she'd done some research on Holt and the Corcoran Team. Not that there was much to find on him, but she'd had some luck on his group.

She walked over to where he stood by the edge, staring out into the yard and across the black water of the small lake fifty feet in front of it. He leaned with his palms resting against the railing. The move had him bending slightly, showing off those shoulders and his very impressive backside.

The faded jeans balancing on those hips. The muscles rippling to the point she could see them through the thin fabric of his T-shirt. She'd never noticed a man's clothes before, but on him she noticed everything.

She stood even with him and listened to the sound of animals scurrying in the dark and the steady brush of leaves blowing in the wind. "So you're always going to be hanging around here when you're not working."

He nodded without looking at her. "For now, pretty much."

Even though his stance appeared relaxed, something about him seemed to be on high alert. She could feel the energy pulse off him. Watch his gaze as he scanned the area from one side to the other.

With him around she felt safe, and that was new. She'd learned early to depend on herself. Not expect anything. Hide and run and adapt. That had been her mantra to the day she found her way back to Justice, Oregon, only a few miles from the place that defined so much of who she was and how she saw the world.

As the months ticked by, exhaustion settled in. She helped other members of New Foundations get out. Laid the groundwork and found them new living arrangements. Through her past had the contacts to change identities and keep them safe.

She'd only worked with a few because breaking the silence barrier at the compound proved almost impossible. She had to wait until someone said something to someone and it filtered through contacts back to her. Then came weeks of secret meetings as she built trust.

The whole strategy could be tedious and never amounted to enough. The campground still loomed.

But last night, for the first time in years, she slept without moving and jerking and waking up every few hours. She wanted to think handling the two armed men who stormed her house had something to do with it, but she knew a large thank-you went to Holt. He'd stayed on her couch and kept his promises. Harm did not come knocking and he did not do anything to scare her.

And now they'd arrived at night number two. "I've decided it's okay for you to stay."

He threw her the side eye before going back to his visual tour of the property in front of them. "You just figured that out now?"

It was amazing how she could start thinking good things about him and working up a warm fuzzy feeling and then he'd talk and—boom— the goodwill fizzled. Communicating did not appear to be where they excelled. "I looked into the Corcoran Team."

He turned then. Stood up and gave her his full attention. "Okay."

"I'm thinking I saw a sanitized version, like the version you and your people were okay with me seeing, but I was able to find some references." After an internet search turned up bland and unhelpful results, she'd called in some favors to help her get through a firewall or two. She had a bit of inside information on the group.

"That's kind of the point. It's hard to work undercover, which we sometimes need to do, if everyone can find your face all over social media."

"Makes sense." And the information she'd found bore that out. The group had taken on huge companies and small governments, the NCIS and government contractors. The only allegiance the members appeared to have was to each other. "Even confirmed your existence on the team with your boss."

That had been an interesting exercise. She'd seen a few references to Connor Bowen, the owner and leader, and to one other member of the team, a former NCIS agent, but no one else. There could be two guys on the team or two hundred and there was no way for her to tell just by searching around.

The wall of secrecy extended to the team's location and exactly what they could do and how much the government knew about their work. There had been exactly one photo, an older one of Connor Bowen. He had the tall, dark and handsome thing down. Looking at Holt, Lindsey wondered if "speech-stealing hot" was some sort of job requirement for this group.

Connor's deep and reassuring voice had matched the confident look he wore in the photo. He hadn't sounded all that shocked about Holt giving away his identity, but Connor had made her repeat three times the part about Holt playing the role of her fake boyfriend. She'd swear he'd laughed.

"Wait a minute." Holt shook his head as if trying to assess what she'd just said. "Connor actually talked with you?"

"Well, finding the number proved impossible. I had to call other agencies and do a bunch of internet searches, all which pointed to the fact the Corcoran Team didn't have a number I could access. To the extent anyone admitted Corcoran even existed. Then right when I gave up, the phone rang and Connor was on the line." The whole thing had a Big-Brother-is-watching feel that freaked her out. "Spooky, by the way."

"Joel tracks all searches for Corcoran. He lets people see only what he wants them to see so he can monitor and do some looking of his own."

She had no idea who that was, but her mind went to a bigger question. "Searches where?"

A faint smile crossed Holt's mouth. "Everywhere."

"The information lockdown is a bit intimidating." She could think of a few more words, but that seemed like the nicest.

"Just as Connor wants it."

"Well, he didn't seem happy about me bugging him, but yes. He answered my questions...sort of." The man had sounded downright stunned when she insisted she needed some sort of verification of Holt's identity. She could only assume other people saw Holt's imposing form and I'm-in-charge swagger and capitulated without a fight.

Not her. If he wanted that kind of woman, she was not his type...not that he served as anything other than a bodyguard for her.

"I filled him in on the status of the assignment an hour ago." Holt started to say something else, then stopped.

"He must have called me right after that." Or at least that was what he'd told her. "Apparently you told him you broke cover."

Holt switched to frowning. Something he excelled at to the point of being an expert. "You're sounding sort of official there."

"I borrowed his phrase." If she could remember more, she'd throw them out, too.

"So now you know I'm legitimate and we can stop arguing about that, right?" Holt's gaze returned to the yard and the shuffling of dirt in the distance.

She shrugged even though the gesture was

wasted. He didn't even give her eye contact. "For now."

Without seeming to move, he angled his body. Stood partway in front of her, blocking her body from the quiet night beyond them. "I'm at a disadvantage here. You know about me and you're not coughing up any details about yourself."

"Noticed that, did you?"

He winked at her. "Don't let the shoulders fool you. I'm not as slow as I look."

That zapped the amusement right out of her. "You're not going to forget I said that, are you?"

"No way."

She rushed to fix her mess. "What I meant was—"

He pinned her in place with a quick glance. "I know what you meant."

The guy could stop looking like that. So determined and…big. He crowded in on her on the large open porch without even moving. Something about the way he held his body and aimed that intense stare had her squirming.

"Clearly you don't have a problem with ego." She wished he taught a class in that, because she'd be in the front row.

"I know mutual attraction when I see and feel it."

"Mutual?" That struck her as such a tame

term for the need that had pulsed through her ever since he arrived in town.

She knew how many times a day her mind wandered and his face popped into her head. From the first time she'd seen him, picking out a muffin and ordering black coffee from the deli she helped manage, her common sense took a nosedive. One look at him and every vow she'd ever made about staying focused on her quest died a withering death.

He shook his head. "You are not going to derail this conversation."

"I can try."

"You might..." His head snapped back in the direction he'd been looking for the past few minutes. Far left behind the shed.

"What is it?" She dropped her voice to a whisper that barely carried over the sound of her breathing.

"Company."

"Are you kidding?" She wanted to scream, shout...find her gun. She went with listening instead. Not her strongest skill, but at least it was something she could control while the world seemed to be bouncing around at random.

"I've been tracking the person for about fifteen minutes."

The constant visual search and the thrum of awareness running through him made sense.

Still, the fact that the guy could chat while conducting surveillance and not show any signs of anxiety confused her. "While we were talking?"

"Then and before."

Well, sure. He acted as if that were normal. "You could warn a person."

"Time to move."

She almost didn't hear the whispered comment, but she did see the change come over him. It was as if he switched from being on watch to back to normal again, which made no sense to her at all.

"I think we should call it a night and go inside." His voice picked up a bit in volume. Not enough to be obvious, but a slight beat or two more than before.

She'd rather go with that gun idea. "Absolutely."

She pitched her voice nice and strong even as her insides shook. The touch of his hand right before he wrapped an arm around her shoulders helped. He guided them through the front door and inside. She didn't remember moving until he shut the door behind her.

He reached down to his ankle and pulled up with a gun in his hand. That was when she noticed he held two. His dark eyes flashed with fire as he morphed from the calm guy standing outside, getting some air, back to the fierce protector. She approved of the change. And she finally got it. The last part had been an act to let whoever lingered out there think he was safe.

He handed her a gun. "You know how to use it?"

"Yes." A whole range of guns. Guns, knives, some explosives. The New Foundations leadership didn't bother with subtleties back when she got stuck up there. You learned how to fight because weak people were useless to the cause. She just never really understood what the cause was supposed to be.

As soon as the gun hit her palm, she checked it. The magazine, the chamber. This weapon didn't belong to her, but she'd be able to pull the trigger. She was not afraid to do what had to be done to protect herself.

Holt positioned her in the doorway between the kitchen and the family room. She had her back against a solid wall and a clear view of the door and a patch of the front yard through the window within her line of sight.

This guy was good. He knew exactly how to keep on the offensive. She didn't think she could find him more attractive, but in that moment she did.

"Stay here." He held out a hand as if to keep her in place even though he never touched her. "Shoot anyone who is not me. Aim for the leg to make him hobble or the hand to make him drop the gun."

That bordered on insulting. "I'm a better shot than that."

"It's a risk to keep the guy breathing, but I need him alive for questioning." Holt delivered his comment and then slipped away from her.

For a big man, he moved without making a sound. Even the floorboards that usually creaked didn't. He shifted and stalked around her furniture and through the room until he disappeared.

She had two choices—sit and wait or track and help. She'd made a vow to step in and not remain silent years ago. She followed it now.

As she reached her kitchen, then the back door of the cottage, she visually searched for him. He'd have to be running to be gone, but she couldn't see him.

He'd congratulated her on her security system, then set up additional sensor lights that afternoon, insisting she had blind spots he needed to fix. One of those popped on behind the shed where she kept the lawn mower and other yard equipment.

She squinted, thinking she'd see movement. She could make out one dark blob...then another. They were nearly on top of each other.

She was halfway outside with the door banging behind her before she remembered Holt's words: stay here.

Chapter Five

Holt heard the door slam a second before the sound of footsteps echoed around him. He focused, trying to pull the sounds apart. He had not one but two people out there with him in the dark. The only good news was that Lindsey was likely one of those people. He liked the odds of him against one attacker, but he hated the idea of her wandering into danger.

He ignored the sound of sneakers slipping against the wet grass and concentrated on what he could handle. Not her, but the man who had been lingering in the yard, hiding behind trees and leaning against the shed, while Holt watched him.

The guy had waited before moving in, but now he hid in that small building. The same one Lindsey said they used for storage. Holt would blow it up or drag him out. Whatever strategy would keep the guy from venturing near Lindsey worked for Holt.

But he had to move because even now she flew across the yard. She moved in a soundless blur. Once she got near him, whatever advantage he now held would be gone because she'd become his priority.

He signaled for her to stop but had no idea if she saw him. He didn't wait.

Weapon up, he slunk around the outside of the building, crouching low and placing careful quiet footsteps. If the attacker shot through the wall, he should miss. Most people shot at standing height. Holt hovered well below that.

By the time he got to the door, Lindsey stood fewer than fifteen feet away. He motioned for her to stop, and this time her forward momentum slammed to a halt. She stood there, frozen.

He didn't suffer from the same problem. He hit the watch alarm to bring Shane and Cam running. They'd come in stealth mode and assess the situation before doing anything that would derail the mission. They'd also make sure nothing happened to Lindsey if something did happen to him.

Then the silent countdown started. After one last glance at Lindsey to reassure himself she hadn't moved, Holt took off. Rounded the corner and hit the doorway with his shoulder. A huge splintering crack ripped through the air around them. Wood shredded and what was left of the door bounced against the inside wall.

Holt caught the bounce with his hip and went in shouting. In two steps he bulldozed over the figure looming on the other side of the door. Momentum kept them moving. Holt didn't stop until he had the man—and by the sheer size this was definitely a man—pinned against the riding lawn mower.

Holt had the guy's back resting on the seat and his feet scraping against the ground as he tried to get his footing. But Holt didn't give him the chance. He had wads of the guy's shirt in his fists as he leaned in.

The guy's fear hit Holt first. Panic and anger all wrapped up in one ball.

He flailed and called out, "Stop!"

The voice registered first. Holt recognized it as one of the attackers from last night. Holt could tie the guy back to the threats he'd overheard, then to the run on Lindsey's house and now to her yard. The repeated shots took guts. It suggested a dangerous level of desperation.

"Grant?" Holt called up the name out of nowhere. Grant was the sidekick type. The guy who led with his fists because he lacked the intuition and skills to be at the top.

Lindsey's foot hit the threshold. Then she rushed inside. "What's going on?"

Time to play the role of disgruntled and concerned boyfriend. Holt didn't have much experience with this, but he was just frustrated enough over Lindsey following him and walking straight into danger that he thought he could fake it. "Go inside."

Grant tried to hold up one of his hands. "I can explain."

Holt used his knee to pin one of Grant's arms down. The steering wheel took care of the other. "Do it now."

"I came looking for you." The words rushed out of Grant as he stumbled to get them out.

"Why?" Holt angled his body so he stayed between Grant and Lindsey.

Grant might be shaking and stuttering now, but that all could be an act. The guy possessed one of those huge lurking frames, as if he could get into uniform and walk onto the front line of any professional football team and fit in. That didn't mean he couldn't fake it all.

"You're supposed to be at the bunkhouse," he said.

This was a new rule. Holt wondered who added it and why. "No one told me about any curfew."

"There isn't…" Grant exhaled as his head dropped back against the metal. "Can you let me up?"

"No." That was just about the last thing Holt planned to do this evening.

Lindsey reached over, coming far too close, and snatched the gun out of the large pocket of Grant's jacket. "I agree. You stay pinned down until you tell us why you're hanging out on my property."

Something about seeing her there, amid the chaos and fighting, snapped Holt back into perspective. He didn't need an arrest tonight. He needed an explanation.

"One more time." Holt eased up on the grip around Grant's neck.

"I can't breathe." He coughed, nearly doubling over.

Holt waited for Grant to stop with the theatrics.

"Again." Never one for an overabundance of words, Holt stuck with that.

"When you're new, the expectation is you'll stay around the bunkhouse. You've been going out and I was asked to make sure you were okay." The guy managed to shrug from his awkward position.

Holt wasn't impressed. From the way Lindsey frowned it didn't look as if she believed the line either.

"How did you know I was here?" Holt asked.

Grant smiled. "The leader sees all."

Now was not the time for enlightenment nonsense. "Try again."

"There are rumors about you and Ms. Pike."

It all sounded rational except that it wasn't. Holt didn't see how there could be gossip about anything, since the whole fake boyfriend thing had only come up last night. "Why not tell me today when we were up at camp?"

Lindsey snorted. "And if your visit is fact-finding and innocent, why not come to my front door?"

Yeah, Holt liked her point even better. "Answer that one."

He eased back so Grant could sit up. When he stopped there, Holt dragged the guy to his feet. He was younger and bigger but needed hours of training to be effective. Despite the time at the campground, from what Holt could see no one had taught Grant or anyone those skills. And Holt had no intention of doing it now.

Grant shrugged. "I didn't know if the rumors were true. I was trying to double-check."

Lindsey made a half-strangled noise. "By looking through windows?"

Holt had known she'd hate that, but the reality check could turn out to be a good thing. She needed to understand the danger and the players. Sometimes novices in matters like this caused the most trouble. He needed her protected and ready. Though the fury pounding off her suggested she could handle herself just fine.

"Maybe we should call in the sheriff," Lindsey said, selling it as if she thought law enforcement might help when she clearly didn't. "He's looking into a break-in here."

"That was not me." Grant held up both hands. "Checking up on you, that's all. I swear."

As if that didn't make it bad enough. Holt had no idea why this kid—and close-up, Holt could see he was just that, maybe in his midtwenties—thought that admission got him anywhere. At camp he was the gung-ho type. Tonight he cowered.

"Did someone tell you to come here?" Holt danced around the main question but wondered if he needed some work on the skills, since Lindsey flinched.

"No." Grant didn't break eye contact. Didn't get fidgety. "It was my idea."

Holt almost wondered if that was true. Anyone with true skills and experience would have come up with something better.

Backing away, Holt gave the guy a bit of breathing room. "I'm with Lindsey."

She frowned at him. "With?"

Holt refused to believe she didn't understand. "Dating."

"You're staying here?" Grant asked the question with a shake in his voice.

"The point is that you do not have her permission or mine to be around here." Holt decided to shake the kid. Dropped his voice low and menacing and shot Grant an expression that promised pain. "If I find you here again I won't need the sheriff. Do we understand each other?"

Grant didn't say anything. Just stood there, wide-eyed and unmoving.

"To be clear." Lindsey kept glaring at Grant. "I'll shoot you."

Holt had to smile at that. "Yes, she will."

"Okay, I get it." Grant swore under his breath. "Stay away."

"Right." Holt stepped back, leaving a slim trail for the guy to escape the shed. "Now go."

Grant didn't hesitate. He bolted around them, smacking into a ladder and running out before Holt could say anything else.

Quiet returned to the property as tension ramped up around them. Holt tried to find the right words to make her understand he was in charge, always and unquestionably.

She faced him. "That went well."

With that the anger whooshed right out of him. Something about seeing her with the gun and knowing she could and would use it if necessary had him relaxing. This woman would not hide under a bed. If threatened she'd come out fighting.

She got hotter with each passing second.

But Grant wasn't the only one who needed to "get" a few points. Holt needed Lindsey to get one major one, as well. "You were supposed to stay put."

"You should know that's not likely to ever happen." She waved a hand in front of him, up and down his torso. "This bossing-people-around thing you do doesn't work for me."

Yeah, she'd made that clear. Looked as though he had to find a new way of handling her, because his usual skill set kept misfiring. "Noted."

"We're in this together."

The words sent an odd sensation spinning through him. One he couldn't pinpoint or identify. "On that subject."

Wariness washed over her, changing everything from her facial expression to her stance. "I almost hate to ask, but what?"

Smart woman. "We're about to get company."

She looked around. "Another attacker?"

"No, but I'd say we have two seconds before you meet the rest of my team." Not that he thought bringing them all together was a great idea. He just didn't have a choice since he'd already sounded the silent alarm.

She tucked her hair behind her ear. "I'm not sure I'm ready."

"From what I've seen, you can handle anything." Including him...which scared him more than he wanted to admit.

SIMON PLANNED ON an evening of research. He had stacks of paperwork on Hank Fletcher. The guy left a trail. A difficult one, which was part of the reason Simon had thought the other man would fit in so well at New Foundations.

Give him a purpose and a home, build his confidence and loyalty. Hand him enough responsibility to feel secure, then begin to plant the seeds. Simon had been using the same system for years.

Some men took longer to convince. Some bought into the program from the beginning. No matter the amount of time it took, Simon won. The days of him waiting and following had long passed.

He had folders sitting on the edge of the desk. The content in front of him highlighted potential recruits. Most of the time people found their way to New Foundations without any help. The disenfranchised and disillusioned.

Every now and then they'd target someone and spend the time luring him or her, usually him, in. Simon set aside time tonight to analyze the people outlined in those folders, but Todd's call interrupted his plans.

Todd and Grant stood in front of his desk. Todd, tall and sure and full of fury, while Grant looked down and shuffled his feet. Simon had heard the report, but he wanted the live version.

"What happened tonight?" When no one talked, Simon's patience slipped. He looked from one to the other and settled on Grant. "Now."

His breath came out in a gasp. Then he started talking. "I went to Ms. Pike's house again."

The words grated across Simon's nerves. His orders had been clear. No one disobeyed his orders. "Why?"

"I thought I could gather some intel." Grant lifted his head and didn't break eye contact. "Show you what I could do."

An interesting idea, but Simon already knew what needed to be done. He did not need assistance from a novice. "What made you think you were qualified to devise strategy?"

Some of the color drained from Grant's face. "I've been trained."

Simon glanced at Todd. "Apparently not well enough, since this is your second failure in two days. Both of you."

So much promise, but Grant continued to be a disappointment. Simon teamed him up with Todd, thinking the match made sense, but Todd taught by yelling and hitting. Grant didn't appear to respond well to that tactic, which was unfortunate.

"Training or not, Hank found you and issued a threat," Todd grumbled.

"I will hear the explanation from Grant." Simon made a mental note that all the men needed a reminder lesson on boundaries. "Continue, Grant."

"I thought I could slip in, watch and report back." Grant shifted around, waved his hand. He'd gone from the collected man who welcomed the assignment of grabbing Lindsey to a man on the edge.

This would not do at all. Simon had no other choice but to make Grant an example. "But you did not ask my permission before acting. You know about the concept of chain of command from your time in the military."

There was no room for independent thinking in this group. They had one leader. One agenda.

"I thought—"

Simon gritted his teeth. "Do not waste my time with justifications."

All the life ran out of Grant. "No, sir."

Seeing the big man humbled in front of him gave Simon an idea. Grant might not be useful as a follower. Somewhere along the line he'd developed this sense that he could make calls, which was absolutely not the case. But that didn't mean he didn't have a use.

"You're dismissed. Go back to the bunk-house." Simon removed the man from his list of concerns with a flick of his hand. He turned to the man he normally could count on to get a job done. "Todd, you stay here."

Todd kept his attention forward, never looking at Grant as he slunk away.

"He lied about leaving. I thought he was going back to the dining hall," Todd said once the door closed behind him.

More excuses. Simon was not in the mood. "He was your responsibility."

"Yes."

"*You* failed me." Words Simon knew would race Todd to the edge of reason.

The man craved acceptance more than most. He'd grown up alone and lost his only home when an injury sidelined him in the middle of his top-tier security career. Simon took him in and invested the time his company refused to give him.

Bottom line: Todd owed him and knew it.

Todd visibly swallowed. "Yes, sir."

"You need to fix this."

Todd nodded. "I can work on his training and impose some discipline on Grant."

It was too late for that now. Simon had other

plans. "Maybe there's another way Grant can help us with Ms. Pike."

Todd frowned. "Sir?"

The more Simon thought it through, the more he liked this alternative. There would be some loss and a need for retraining, but he'd get a lot more in return. "It's time to send Lindsey Pike a message."

Todd's frown didn't ease. "Okay."

"We'll use Grant to do it." Then she would be right where Simon wanted her—trapped.

Chapter Six

Lindsey left home the next morning well before dawn. Holt had laid down all sorts of rules and regulations the night before. Talked about the places she could go and how she needed a bodyguard with her at all times. Generally bossed and pushed, even threatened to take her gun.

Not her favorite characteristics in a guy.

She'd nodded, gone to bed and beat him out of the house that morning. She knew he'd have to use the bathroom sometime. When he did, she took off on her hour-long drive into the mountains. She had a feeling the note of explanation she left would not make her return run any smoother.

She turned into the unpaved drive and went as far as she could in a car. The path led to a small cabin tucked into a round of towering trees. This place didn't have an official address. She'd discovered the hard way on a previous visit that it didn't have a working bathroom.

None of that mattered. She needed to see the man inside. Roger Wallace, nineteen in age but far younger than that in terms of social skills. He'd spent years at New Foundations. He'd moved in there with his uncle long after she got out. He was her first rescue. And he'd missed two check-ins.

She turned off the car and parked it by the gate. Once again she took out the burner phone and made the call. Left the emergency code... then waited. After a few minutes ticked by with no reply, she started walking. This was not the place one traveled without an invitation, but she knew the markers.

Before she rounded the first turn, she heard it. The rumble of an engine and the crunch of tires over gravel. Relief raced through her. Glancing back, she expected to see Roger's beat-up truck. Instead of blue with a smashed-in front fender, she saw a familiar black. Clean and shiny with Holt taking up the front seat.

She winced. Actually winced. Then she saw the expression on his face and had to fight the temptation to step back.

He slammed the door and stalked up the path toward her. Stepped over the gate without breaking stride and headed right for her. She knew she needed to shout out a warning about booby traps, but she doubted he'd hear her over the anger whirling around him. He came at her in a straight line, his attention never wavering and his frown growing more severe with each step.

She jumped on the offensive. "How did you find me?"

"No, Lindsey." He stopped right in front of her with his hands on his hips and the fury radiating off him. "We aren't doing it this way."

She could hear the tremble of anger in his voice. Not that the eyes flashing with fire didn't give him away.

But something about him verbally throwing elbows and insisting on always getting his way put her on the edge. He used that tone, and her immediate reaction was to deny him whatever he demanded. Since that felt juvenile and they did wade deeper into danger with every step, she treaded carefully. Went with a stall. "I have no idea what you mean."

"You were attacked."

She hadn't exactly forgotten. "I remember."

"Do you?" His voice stayed deadly soft.

She inhaled, pushing out her natural impulse to fight back, and tried to regain her control. Roger could be in trouble, and having Holt there might not be a terrible thing, now that he was already standing right there. "I'll explain if you calm down."

"You will explain even if I start shouting."

Holt wasn't exactly making it easy to take the high road. She did it anyway. "Roger hasn't checked in."

Holt didn't say anything for a second. Just stared at her while the deep frown lines on his face eased. Not much but a bit. "I need more details."

She toyed with the idea of telling him only enough to clue him in but not enough to over-share about Roger. She abandoned the idea as soon as she thought it. This wasn't the time. Knowing too much might endanger Roger's cover, but Holt possessed a protection power she didn't and she had to trust he would step up.

She stuck to the facts and recited them as if reading from a file. "Roger Wallace, a former resident at New Foundations. He lives out here. We have a check-in schedule and he missed it."

"How many times?"

She didn't pretend to misunderstand. Holt was collecting details and she appreciated the need. "Two."

"Has it ever happened before?"

Roger worked with her. He provided the information she needed to help others. He had trouble adjusting, but he could walk former members through the necessary life skills and he had volunteered to do that.

That meant she stayed in constant contact with

Roger. Three days without a word was two days too long. They had a mandatory check-in time every other day. He'd never missed one. "No."

Holt's arms finally dropped to his sides. "We'll get back to the part about how you know him and who he is to you later."

That was exactly what she didn't want. "I don't think—"

"But right now we're going to check on him." Holt walked past her.

She grabbed his arm and dragged him to a halt. "Stop."

"Lindsey, do not test me. I am trying not to unleash on you for running out without telling me." He didn't pull out of her hold. His jaw had also unclenched.

She took that all as a good sign. "You would have insisted I not come here."

"Right." He jerked as if he wanted to take off again.

"Holt, stop." The man's stubborn nature made her head pound. "You are walking into danger."

"You're saying he'll shoot if he sees me?" Holt didn't seem all that concerned about the possibility.

From only a few days with him, she guessed he thought he could take on a bullet and win. Sometimes she wondered. The guy did possess this amazing sense of confidence. She watched him and felt safe and secure.

But there were explosives rigged and planted along the route to the house. She could look up and see it ahead, but getting there required twists and turns. Taking Roger out of the camp didn't change his us-against-them mind-set. "If you even get that far. He's got a system of traps out here."

"Then we're leaving." The news didn't faze him at all. He listened, nodded and reevaluated. "It's that simple."

She loved that about him. She threw roadblock after roadblock at him and he didn't shake. She'd never known a man like him. Her father had been weak and easy to turn. He'd heard about New Foundations and viewed it as some Nirvana. A place they could go and be safe.

"I know where the explosives are." She pointed to random spots on the ground. But they were only random if you didn't know the pattern. She did.

"We still need to go."

The words came out strong and sure, but a strange emotion moved over his face. She guessed the rescuer inside him battled with the guy who got the job done. She tried to make the fight a bit easier. "First, I'm attacked and now Roger missed a check-in."

Holt studied her. "You think he's in trouble."

"I know he is."

He nodded and stepped in closer. "Tell me about the booby traps."

She turned over his hand and traced a pattern on his palm. "The explosives are buried in an 'x' with a set of devices in the middle of the drive in a line from that tree." She pointed at a strange bush with red-brown leaves planted among the thick growth. A shock of color among all that green.

"Got it."

She knew he would, so she told him all of it. "There are trip wires and I don't know what else throughout the woods. If we stick to the path and use clues, mainly those posts, we'll be fine."

"You've done this before."

That didn't mean it didn't scare her, because it did. "I visit Roger in person out here every few weeks."

"Did you rescue him from the campground?" Holt's eyes narrowed. "Is that the big secret? Is that why someone up there wants to grab you?"

The reminder sent a tremble spinning through her. "Is now the right time for that discussion?"

"Probably not but it's happening later." He exhaled. "I don't like this."

"Because you insist on leading and hate not to be in charge?" But she knew that meant he agreed to go forward. Holt wasn't the type to run away from a potentially dangerous situation. Neither was she. Not anymore.

He glared at her. "Add that to the list of things we're going to argue about later."

She had a feeling he wouldn't forget that awful future conversation he kept referencing…unfortunately. "For the record, I'm not really looking forward to this discussion."

"You drew the battle line when you left that note." He scoffed. "You actually thought telling me not to worry would work?"

She couldn't really argue with any of his anger or her bad choices. She'd operated this morning as she always did, head down and moving forward. She acted alone because that was what she knew.

Getting used to having him around would take time. But the bigger concern was that she'd get accustomed to him being around just as he decided it was time to go.

No question she stood on the edge of heartache. She knew and saw the warning signs and didn't know how to avoid the danger.

"See those?" She pointed to the faded ribbons tied high up in the tree, then followed the nearly invisible line of wire toward the ground.

"Traps."

It had taken her forever to understand Roger's

system. She talked tough, but Roger came out and walked her into the cabin almost every time she visited. "You recognize the setup?"

"Of course."

Of course. "Normal people aren't familiar with explosive devices."

The tightness around Holt's mouth finally eased. "I don't think we know the same people."

She started walking. "I don't—"

"No." He grabbed her back. Wrapped an arm around her waist and pulled her tight against his chest before she got more than a few feet away from him. "Do not put your foot down."

She looked a few steps in front of her and saw the disturbance in the rocks and dirt. Squinting, she noticed the thin wire. Tiny, almost a line in the dirt, but she recognized it. Not in this fashion, maybe, but Roger had shown her examples. She'd almost shuffled her way over a trip wire.

Her heartbeat thundered in her ears as she kept her death grip on his arm. "That wasn't supposed to be there."

As if she weighed less than a pillow, Holt tightened his hold and lifted her. He stepped back, taking them both out of the immediate danger of the wire.

The second those muscled arms enfolded her, the fear subsided. Her breath hiccupped out of her and she grabbed on. When he lowered her feet to the ground again, her knees buckled. All the strength left her muscles, and a sudden dizziness hit her. The mix of fear and relief had her leaning into him.

He glanced down at her with eyes filled with concern. "You okay?"

"Not really." Not when her bones had turned to jelly.

"Looks like your friend changed the pattern."

But that was the point. That didn't happen. Roger wouldn't put her at risk. He also wouldn't impose a communication blackout. The longer she stood there, the more worried she grew. "He wouldn't."

Holt didn't let go of her. Strong hands held on to her forearms, keeping her balanced. "This isn't like in the movies, Lindsey. You step on that and it explodes. There's no click or chance to defuse it. It will go off."

"I both hate and am grateful that you know that." And he seemed to know everything. When it came to fighting and surviving, he was the man she wanted by her side.

"We're changing this."

But he needed to understand she had an obligation to Roger. One she took seriously. She thought of him as a friend, though she wasn't sure if Roger knew how to have those. At the very least, he worked with her and she cared about him. She had to know he was safe. "We can't go back."

"Agreed. We need to see this through now." He stepped around her until she faced his back. "Follow behind me. Hook your finger through my belt loop and match your steps to mine. I lift my foot and you put yours in the exact same place."

This wasn't fair. She should take the risk, not him. But the determination in his voice suggested she not even try to argue the point. "Fine."

"We'll go slow."

And they did. It felt as if hours passed as they walked up the drive. More like lumbered. He measured every step and constantly scanned the area. Sometimes minutes ticked by between moves. Once or twice he shuffled his feet.

With every placement of his foot he made a mark. She guessed that was his form of leaving bread crumbs for them to find their way back again. Tedious or not, the process worked.

They got to the front of the cabin and she finally unclenched her fingers from his belt loops.

Instead of a feeling of relief and being ready to go, dread washed over her. The usual broken and cracked pots filled his porch, but there was no sign of Roger. His truck sat in its spot. She never quite understood how he got that thing in there, through the tangle of branches and over the explosives, but he did and refused to share the secret.

"This is bad." She whispered the comment before she could think it through. Didn't even know she was saying it until it spilled out. "The lack of gunfire."

"The front door is open."

She followed his gaze and stared at the green door. Didn't see anything wrong with it. "You can tell?"

"It's not lining up with the trim." He pointed as he talked. "I also see a trip wire at the top of the stairs. Is that normally there?"

"No, but how in the world can you—"

"Perfect eyesight and expensive training." Holt glanced around the wooded area one last time before turning to her. "Call for him."

"Roger?" She shouted his name two more times. Birds fluttered in the trees at the sound of her voice, but nothing and no one else moved. He didn't come out and threaten, which was what she expected him to do if he saw a stranger with her. He might even fire a warning shot first.

Holt swore and mumbled something about sleeping in. "Does this Roger have any friends he could be visiting?"

That was an easy one. "No."

"Let's go this way." Instead of walking up

the front steps as she expected, as any regular person would do, Holt took them around to the side of the porch. He crouched down and peered under the slats. Used a stick he found on the ground to tap different sections of the wood. Whatever he saw or heard must have satisfied him, because he held out a hand to boost her up onto the railing. "Here."

Going first made her stomach tumble, and not in the good way. She feared setting her foot down the wrong way or putting too much weight on one board over another. So she sat there and waited for Holt to pop up over the side. He did and kept going. Straddled the railing and headed for the door with careful steps.

Holt pivoted around pots filled with dirt and others set up in what looked like a haphazard grouping but really served as yet another warning system for Roger. "Do you see anything out of the ordinary for this guy?"

She knew the place looked as if it had been left in disarray, but this was how it always looked to her. The tickling sensation at the back of her neck proved to be the bigger issue. She didn't ignore her body's panic signals. Not anymore.

She guessed Holt operated on what he could see and understand, but she told him the truth anyway. "No, but it doesn't feel right."

"I think we should follow your gut on this one." He delivered the surprise statement, then held out a hand to her. "Stay behind me and watch the path."

The comment and the feel of his palm against hers had barely registered when he pushed the door open. He didn't need to turn the knob. A gentle touch sent it swinging.

He took half a step and froze. "Damn."

"What?" She peeked over his shoulder and immediately regretted it. Her gaze went to the blob on the floor. Dark and huge, the stain grew as she watched. Then the reality hit her as a buzzing started in her head. "Is that…"

She couldn't say the word. Not when she was too busy trying not to heave.

"If I had to guess, I'd say blood." Holt squeezed her hand, then let go. "And too much of it."

She watched him reach for his phone. He pressed in a few numbers, then disconnected. Then he started taking photos.

Every choice struck her as sick and wrong. None of the callous indifference matched the man she'd seen in action over the past few days.

She grabbed his arm, thinking to spin him around. He didn't move while he shifted in front of her. "What are you doing?"

"I called in Cam and now I'm preserving the scene until he gets here."

None of the words made sense in her head. "What?"

"Cam is one of my men. You were supposed to meet him the other night but they—he and Shane—followed Grant back to the campground instead."

'I remember.'

"We need experts to sift through the clues before Sheriff Carver and his band of misfits come storming in here." Holt didn't even blink. "Cam and Shane qualify as experts."

Just thinking about what could have happened to Roger and the need for more men started the world spinning. She reached out to lean against the doorway and spied a flannel shirt rolled up in a ball near her foot. "This is his—"

Holt stopped her before she could pick it up. "Don't touch anything."

"Evidence?"

"Or more traps. I don't know what we're looking at here."

Holt managed to lose her again. Seemed obvious to her. "A crime scene."

"Probably." He pointed at the lamp turned on its side and the couch cushions tossed and sitting at strange angles. "I'm trying to figure out if it looks staged."

A memory came zipping back. The car accident and the blood. How Roger siphoned off his own and saved it for weeks. "Oh."

Holt's gaze shot right to her. "Tell me."

"He faked his own death to get out of New Foundations." That was only a fraction of the weirdness. She delivered the rest. "I helped him do it. That's the mission that binds me to this area when I really want to move as far away as possible."

Holt being Holt, he didn't show much emotion. A deeper frown, maybe, but nothing in the way of shock. "I figured as much."

She'd told him this huge secret. A piece of information that should have unraveled who he thought she was and raised all sorts of questions. "That's all you have to say?"

He nodded. "When we talk later, that will be one of the topics."

That was starting to look like a really long future conversation. But she couldn't think about that now. Could barely think about anything as she stood there, trying to fight off the need to double over and try to catch her breath. "What now?"

"We back out and let my men check the scene. They'll grab anything that implicates you or points to Roger's past, since I'm thinking you want all that hidden."

She didn't fight it. "Yes."

"Then do not move." He took one step, and an agonizing creak rang out under his heel. "I mean it."

"I plan on listening to you from now on."

His eyes narrowed. "I want to believe you."

She didn't touch that. Watched him travel around the small two-room space instead. He conducted a visual tour of each surface and snapped photos before coming back to stand next to her. "There's no body. Plenty of signs of a struggle but no drag marks in or out."

She had no idea how he picked all that up in a two-minute visual scan. "That's a horrible sentence."

"I don't disagree." He glanced at his watch. "Time to go."

She didn't question him, mostly because she didn't want to stand in the middle of the macabre scene with the ransacked cabin and the papers strewn everywhere. And the blood. She might see that puddle every day for the rest of her life.

He made it sound easy, but retracing their steps took almost as long as getting to the cabin. It probably didn't help that she'd turned into a shaking mess. What little she was able to hold it together back at Roger's house abandoned her the farther away she got. A trembling started deep in her bones and moved through her entire body.

By the time she got back to her car and tried to pull out her keys, she was a mess. She dropped the set twice. The third time they jangled so loudly in her palm that Holt removed them with a gentle touch. When he suggested she ride with him and he have his men, whoever they were, return her car, she jumped at it.

The long drive back to her house passed in slow sections. She dreaded he'd start that conversation he was so desperate to have. But he didn't. He turned on the heat, despite the time of year, and let the radio play softly in the background.

It took until they'd almost reached home for her to realize this qualified as his attempt to put her at ease. He didn't rapid-fire questions at her or demand answers. He let her do battle with the adrenaline coursing through her.

She was about to thank him when she saw the man. Tall and almost as sturdy as Holt. This guy had light brown hair but stood in a battle position that was now so familiar to her—legs apart and hands on hips as the perfect scowl formed on his lips.

The man was handsome and muscular. Very fit. Had a bit of a boyish-charm look to him, while Holt wore that stern countenance a lot of the time. Still, she couldn't help thinking this guy and Holt knew each other. "Who is that?"

"He's with me." Holt parked the car and turned off the engine. "And it's very bad he's here."

That was the last thing she wanted to hear. She tried to form a question, but nothing came out. She used up all her energy opening the door and somehow getting out.

"What's up?" Holt frowned and walked at the same time. "You're supposed to be out with Cam conducting some forensics on that cabin."

"Ma'am." The guy nodded at her before returning his full attention to Holt. "We have a new problem."

Holt swore in a voice just above a whisper. "Another one?"

"What is it?" Lindsey asked at the same time.

The guy looked at her then. "There's a dead body on your property."

Chapter Seven

So many questions bombarded Holt's brain. He wanted to know more about this Roger person and how he'd got out of the camp. Holt also needed more insight into Lindsey. He wanted to sleep with her. Kiss her, touch her, hold her in bed and talk with her. His sudden need for that last one made him twitchy, but there was so much about her, her life and this situation he didn't know.

Walking now between her and Shane struck Holt as strange. He'd introduced them and watched as they shook hands. Holt ignored the "nice job" man-to-man look Shane shot him.

They'd been friends for a long time. They'd known each other and served together for a short stint. Now they worked on the same team, spent a lot of their free time hanging out and had the same goals.

They also shared a similar sensibility about relationships. Neither wanted one. Cam had been with them right up until the point he'd met Julia and then lost his mind.

Holt had watched as the men of Corcoran—the toughest guys either of them knew—get ripped apart by their love for their women. Strong, intelligent men shredded and a mess as they ran around trying to get these amazing women back.

Holt and Shane joked about it. It was embarrassing and Holt didn't want any part of it.

The idea of being vulnerable for a woman, of putting everything on the line, had him mentally throwing up a wall. He liked all the women his friends ended up with and understood why the guys loved them. The matches made sense.

It was the wall of fire they walked through to be together that made no sense to Holt. Why would anyone willingly take that on? He'd never met any woman who turned him around and had him thinking that would be a good idea.

But then he met Lindsey.

She counted as a wild card. He'd never known anyone like her. Even now, as they walked the line of the property and closed in on a section by the water, Holt's mind rolled. He thought back to the things she'd said and the way she acted in danger. So in charge yet human. The combination had him dropping to his knees.

Not that he planned to let either of the people with him know. He'd rather welcome the silence.

"It's Roger," she whispered into the silence.

"We don't know that." Though Holt did think it had to be. A person didn't lose that much blood and live to talk about it. He might have faked his death before, but this was another level.

Shane pushed the branches aside and kept walking. Didn't say anything, as if leaving them to hold a private conversation even though he hovered right there.

She shook her head. "I should have checked in on him sooner."

Without thinking, Holt reached over and took her hand. Slipped his fingers through hers and felt the coolness of her skin and the jumpiness of her raw nerves. She jerked at the contact but didn't let go. No, she tightened her hand around his and held on.

Since he couldn't think of anything smart to say and since he spent part of the time scanning the surroundings for signs of trouble, he figured silence was the best solution anyway. As they got closer to the lake's small shore, Holt saw the body. Crumpled in a heap as the water lapped over his legs.

Definitely a male and not a small one. His face was turned away and the body appeared to be soaked through, either from the night's rain or being in the lake. Too hard to tell without more tests. But Holt was looking at a large form wearing dark clothes, which described a lot of men in this part of Oregon.

Lindsey stopped. Holt didn't notice until he almost yanked hard on her arm. He dropped her hand and turned to her. Shane wore an expression of concern and Holt guessed he had one of his own.

He watched the color drain from her cheeks and he leaned in closer to make sure she didn't pass out or something equally bad. "What is it?"

"That's not Roger."

"That's good news, isn't it?" Shane asked.

Holt wasn't so sure. Roger as the victim made sense. They could make those connections and draw those lines. A dead stranger on her property brought up more questions and increased the danger level.

Holt preferred to fight against a known quantity. Someone with an agenda—revenge, greed, a cause or whatever—could be trapped if you found the right bait. Not so easy with the unknown.

Rather than guess, Holt snapped into action. He walked over to the body, careful not to disturb the scene more than necessary, and crouched down. His gaze traveled, looking for signs of injury other than the obvious gunshot wound to the back of the guy's head. Any identification would help, though the lake had likely carried that away.

He got his phone out, prepared to take photos and prints and send them back to Connor for analysis. When his gaze landed on the dead guy's face, Holt knew he didn't need to worry about the identification. His mind raced as he went through every interaction and conversation. He remembered the threats the last time they'd met.

One thing was clear, their lives were about to explode. Blow right out into the open. So much for Lindsey wanting to live under the radar. Those days might be over. Holt just hoped his cover held long enough to figure all this out.

He motioned for Shane to bring Lindsey closer.

She walked in measured steps with her hand locked on Shane's arm as she stumbled over the loose rocks. "What is it?"

"Not what, who." Holt stood up. "Grant."

"The guy that attacked you at the house and then you caught sneaking around?" Shane made a hmmphing sound as he dropped down to conduct his own visual inspection of the body.

"Gunshot to the back of the head," Holt said, stating the obvious.

Shane glanced up at Lindsey. "Holt said you're a good shot. Where's your gun?"

"At the house." She tore her attention away from the lifeless body and glared at Shane. "Do you think I did it?"

"No, but others might." Holt understood where Shane was going with his thinking and mentally followed along. This scene had all the hallmarks of a trap.

"Why would I kill this guy?" She yelled the question loud enough for her voice to carry through the trees. The steady clap of the water against the rocks played in the background as the breeze blew through, but she stood perfectly still.

Shane stood up. "Someone will have a theory."

"Meaning?" Some of the confidence left her voice.

Never one to mince words, Shane didn't do it now either. "You're about to be set up."

"That's ridiculous." Lindsey snorted. When the men continued to stand there, she looked to Holt, who nodded. "Wait, you agree?"

Holt realized he'd have to spell it out. This was a delicate balance between keeping her calm and telling her what she needed to do so she could act. Unfortunately, he didn't do delicate. "I think Grant here got on the wrong side of someone at the campground. Maybe this is payment for not grabbing you the other night."

"Okay." She made the word last for three syllables.

He could see she still didn't get it. Her brain probably rebelled because of all the violence she'd seen. He couldn't blame her for shutting down. Normal people didn't think things through, looking for every evil angle. "And now he's on your property."

"It's a message or the beginning of a trap, maybe both," Shane said, speaking slower and softer than usual. He didn't do delicate either, but he possessed more tact, which might help in this situation.

For a second Lindsey stared at the rhythmic falling of the small waves before turning back to Holt. "So, what do we do?"

"Go look for your gun and—"

Shane scoffed at that. "I'll bet you a thousand dollars it's not where you think it is."

She shook her head. "I have a security system."

"So?" Shane practically laughed. "I won't tell you how easy it is to manipulate and get around those."

So much for tact. Holt ignored the interruptions and got the rest of his thought out. "Then we call Deputy Carver."

Now he stood back and waited for Lindsey's reaction. He predicted it wouldn't be great. Not that he could blame her. They'd hit her with one bad piece after another. Anyone would buckle.

Instead of screaming the tall trees down around them, she shook her head. "He's useless."

Holt counted on that. Competency meant finding clues and solving the crime, and if someone really was leading law enforcement in Lindsey's direction, Holt needed to slow that progress down. He needed someone who lingered a step behind, and the deputy seemed like the man for the job. "Let's hope so, because I have a feeling we're going to need someone who's not smart enough to follow obvious clues."

Lindsey rolled her eyes. "Frank Jr. is perfect, then."

"Interesting reaction." Shane frowned. "Sounds like a town called Justice doesn't have much of it."

Holt couldn't agree more. "Which is why we're here to help."

SIMON TOOK ONE look at Deputy Carver and thought it was almost unfair how easy the next few minutes were going to be. The elder Carver was someone Simon understood well. He had a singular focus and knew the world didn't always break down into easily definable categories of right and wrong. He could not be managed, but his young son could be.

The young deputy was about to fall into a

pile of trouble if he didn't obey the simple rules. Simon motioned for him to take a seat.

"What is it?" Simon asked after growing weary of Frank just standing there, twisting his hands together.

"There's been some trouble on the Pike property."

Simon knew all about the body and the chaos. Lindsey would no longer be able to hide, which was exactly the point of the exercise. "We've talked about the pros and cons of you coming to my office during the day."

"I followed all the requirements you put in place. No one thinks I'm here on official business. I made it clear this was a social call."

Always nice to have rule-abiding people on his payroll. Simon got a special kick out of taking his relationship with Frank Sr. one generation down and influencing the son, as well. Some people proved easy to purchase. "Tell me about Lindsey Pike."

Frank Jr. lowered his arms and balanced his hands on the back of the chair in front of him. "There's been a murder and it impacts you."

Little slowed Simon down. This wouldn't either. "How?"

"The victim is Grant."

No surprise there. Simon had given the order.

He was just grateful this one had been carried out. "Tell me exactly what you're saying."

"Someone shot Grant in the back of the head and dumped his body next to the waterline near Lindsey's cottage."

Simon didn't care about this news. It didn't impact him at all, except as he could use it to get what he wanted from Lindsey. "What did she see?"

The deputy frowned but was smart enough not to ask too many questions. "Nothing."

"And Hank?" They'd likely serve as alibis for each other. That didn't mean they weren't in it together. Or at least that was the seed he intended to plant...right now.

The deputy shook his head, as if trying to understand the question. "You know about those two?"

The profound lack of faith in him and his skills had Simon thinking he needed to show more strength. So few people even saw him outside camp. Inside he'd become a figurehead and an inspiration, both an example and an ongoing threat. "I know about everyone on my payroll. Every detail. Every secret they don't want me to know."

"There'll be an investigation."

They'd finally hit on a point that interested

Simon. He leaned back in his chair. "Does Lindsey have an alibi?"

Frank Jr.'s hands tightened on the chair until his fingers turned red. "Excuse me?"

"I've heard she's an expert shot." The woman's skills in running and hiding proved impressive, but those days were coming to an end.

"As are a lot of people around in this county, including people who live on your property."

Simon couldn't afford to let the deputy's mind wander in that direction. "I wasn't going to mention this, but Grant had a problem at her house."

"Meaning?"

Just as expected, he took the bait. Simon had to bite back his smile of satisfaction. "He went over there to deliver some information to Hank about work. Hank and Lindsey took exception. They threatened him."

Frank Jr. leaned forward. "What did they say?"

"I wasn't there. I just got the impression Hank made the usual guy threats about staying away from his woman, but Lindsey...well..." Simon tapped his pen against the armrest. Drew out the scene, letting the deputy come to him for each morsel.

"What?"

"She threatened to shoot Grant."

The deputy's head snapped back. "Why would she?"

"I found out, too late, I might add, that Grant had a bit of a crush on her. He's been following her around, or I guess I should use past tense." Simon shook his head to complete the effect. "If I had known, I might have been able to turn this around before it became a tragedy."

The deputy pushed off from the chair and stood up straight again. "You mean Grant was stalking her."

"Nothing on that level. But you can imagine what the news about her dating Hank did to Grant."

"Did he say he was afraid of Hank?"

A reasonable assumption and Simon stored that information away for later. He could push the thinking in that direction if needed, but for now he wanted the spotlight on Lindsey. All the pressure on her. "More like afraid of Lindsey."

Frank Jr. nodded, looking every bit in charge and more like his father than ever. "I'll look into it."

Simon held up his hands. "That's all I'm asking."

Chapter Eight

Hours after the police left and the van took Grant's body away, Lindsey paced her bedroom. The night had fallen and the house had gone to sleep. It was almost two in the morning and she couldn't close her eyes without seeing Grant's limp form. He'd scared her and come at her with a gun, but she hadn't wished him dead. She just wanted to be left alone.

Right now she needed to research or watch mindless television or do something to fill her head with something other than images of blood and gunshot wounds. Normally she'd wander into her family room and do things to keep her busy. Not tonight. Not with two men sacked out on her couch and floor.

After the awful day and all those questions from the deputy she almost felt bad about shutting down on Holt and asking for a few minutes alone. Those minutes turned into hours and now she hovered on the edge of going stir-crazy.

Her in the room with the big bed. Two big men trapped in her small family room with all her extra pillows and blankets, not that they seemed to care about the cramped quarters or lack of amenities. She thought there was probably a better solution, but she couldn't figure it out.

Well, that wasn't true. She knew what she wanted. Holt in here with her.

She thought it and two seconds later she heard a soft knock at her door. After a quick look down at her shorts pajamas, a pink version of the ones Holt had already seen, she reached over and turned the knob. Holt stood there wearing a T-shirt and boxers and nothing else. He had a gun in his hand and stared at her.

"Are you okay?" His voice was filled with concern.

She tried to think back to the past few minutes. She hadn't knocked anything over. She half wondered if she'd started talking out loud. It wouldn't be the first time. She considered it more or less a hazard of living alone. "Why?"

"You're walking around in here." He made a circle in the air with his finger. "Like, nonstop."

She glanced at her bare feet and curled her pink toenails under. There was no way she'd made enough noise to bring her armed bodyguards running. "You could hear that?"

His gaze dropped. Bounced down her body,

then right back up again. "I'm aware of everything you do."

"That sounds odd." But not bad. The tone and words had her body warming from the inside out.

He blew out a long breath. "If you're okay I'll go."

"Stop." She caught his arm before he could execute the great escape. Without using any force, she had him turned around again. His eyebrows rose, but he didn't say anything, so she jumped back into talking. "You can stay for a few minutes."

He looked at the bed, then at her again. "I'm not sure that's a good idea."

The sudden need for him overwhelmed her. She craved his presence. But she knew where his mind went. Hers drove there, too, but she mulled the possibilities over and arrived at a different conclusion.

She wanted him in here, with her. Tonight she needed comfort and reassurance, two things she'd blocked from her life for so long.

Dragging anyone else into her mess struck her as unfair. She lived with danger just out of reach but always waiting there to strike. Lately, it had walked right up to her door. The long hours of research and all the secrets. Sharing even a portion of that made anxiety churn deep in her belly.

But with Holt something changed. He knew danger, lived mired in it and didn't flinch. He would be the type to listen and help her meet her goal...after he lectured her to death about safety. Even with his hotness factor shooting off the charts, he came with some downsides. A stubbornness that matched hers was one.

She stepped back and held out a hand to him. "Just for a few minutes."

He seemed to hesitate, but at least he lowered his gun. "What exactly do you want me to do here?"

Being bold meant taking risks. She didn't do that in her personal life. She'd step right out on the line when it came to doing battle with New Foundations. She fought behind the scenes, but she did fight.

Romance, dating, all that took a backseat. Her experience was limited and she hadn't even been attracted to a man on any physical level in more than a year except for the usual "he's pretty cute" thoughts when she saw some guys around at times.

Still, she jumped in this time knowing he could turn her down and make every second of whatever time they had left together awkward. But from the heat banked in his eyes, she guessed he wouldn't. "Lie down with me until I fall asleep."

His features softened. "Are you scared? Because nothing is going to happen in this house with Shane and me here."

She knew that. When he'd promised her earlier that she wouldn't be arrested right there and then and dragged away from him, she believed that, too. He wanted her safe. She got that.

Whether she amounted to nothing more than a potential witness to him, she didn't know. But he meant more to her. He'd become a symbol of how things could be. Decent and strong. Most of the men she'd known in her life failed at both of those.

She didn't lower her hand. Not yet. "Please."

His gaze jumped back to the mattress before landing on her face again. "For a few minutes only, because I need to keep watch."

As excuses went, that was a strong one. She ignored it anyway. "Thanks."

He unloaded his weapon, then double-checked it before putting it on the table next to her bed. She was going to tell him about the drawer and the small gun safe in there until she remembered him searching through everything in the room with her once they found her gun missing.

Another fact that she could not think about right now. If she added up all the problems of the tragedies of the past few days, she might have to curl up in a ball in the corner. If her mind turned to Roger and what possibly happened to him, she froze.

She didn't have many friends, choosing instead to keep people at a distance and out of harm's way. She cared about Roger. He might not be able to articulate his feelings for her, but she knew he depended on her, and for him that meant something. And she might have failed him.

Holt turned back to her and took her hand. "Lindsey?"

She shook her head, pushing out all the negatives and concentrating on the one positive thing that had happened to her—him. "Sorry."

"Are you nervous?" When she shook her head, he frowned. "You're not afraid of me, are you?"

The conversation had sure gone sideways in the past few seconds. When her thoughts started spinning, he'd shifted into worry mode. She wanted him to back out of it. "I wouldn't want you with me if I were. Truth is, you make me feel safe…and other things."

He nodded but instead of leading her to the bed, he pulled her in close. "We're going to do this first. Get it out of the way so it's not hanging out there between us."

Before she could ask what he was talking about, he lowered his head and his mouth covered hers. The kiss seared through her from the start. Hot and full of need, it pulled her under. Heat enveloped them as his hands found her lower back and hers went to his shoulders. Fingers speared through his soft hair as their lips met again and again.

Something welled inside her. It felt like power and excitement. An intoxicating blend. She couldn't get close enough as her mouth traveled over his.

After a minute of touring and tasting each other, he broke away, panting. Heavy breaths blew through her hair as he rested his cheek against hers. "That may have been a mistake."

She could feel his erection press into the space between her legs. A fresh rush of warmth raced through her. "Felt pretty good to me."

"Too good." He stepped back, putting a few inches of air between them. "That's the point."

For a second she thought he was going to leave, but he leaned down and pulled the covers back. "Get in."

She didn't hesitate. She scurried inside, letting the soft sheets fall around her. She was about to say something to him, give him an out, when he slid in beside her. One turn and he lay behind her with an arm around her waist. His mouth lingered in her hair and a now familiar bulge pressed against her.

"You're safe with me." The words vibrated in

his chest as he spoke them. "Always. You can count on that."

She knew what he was saying. He'd keep her safe but he also wouldn't make a move tonight. The last part both settled and unsettled her. Shane was asleep right outside the door, and the walls were on the thin side. Noises would carry. Then there was the harsh reality of bad timing and the fact that getting involved with Holt would amount to a huge mistake.

All the right answers and items in the "no" column. Still… "I like you holding me."

"Anytime." He laughed. A rich, gruff sound. "Does that sound cheesy?"

"The exact opposite."

She snuggled in, letting her muscles relax as she balanced against him. She should close her eyes and fall off to sleep. Let the poor guy grab a few minutes of rest. But even in the warm wrap of comfort a restlessness churned inside her. For the first time ever she felt the need to spill. To unburden herself.

She fought it off for minutes. Opened her mouth, then closed it and started to fight again.

"You can tell me about whatever has you fidgeting." He squeezed her tighter in a touch so comforting.

Two more minutes of quiet passed, then… "He took me there after the divorce, to New Foundations." The words tumbled out before she could stop them. "Mom got custody, but my father put me in a car during a visitation and drove me away. Stopped to pick up his brother and then we all kept going."

"How old were you?" There was no judgment or surprise in his voice.

"Seven." She kept her eyes open because closing them invited the mental images. "I remember the surroundings turning from sunshine and palm trees to miles without houses or stores."

She'd ridden in the backseat and listened to them talk. Put her hand against the window, and instead of feeling the usual heat, coldness greeted her. Then she saw snow on the ground. She'd begged them to call her mom, and that only agitated her dad more, which started her uncle yelling. He called her ungrateful and blamed her for their move.

The drive went from talk about this big adventure where she got a new name, any one she wanted, to yelling and threatening. Her crying only made it all worse. Her uncle Walt grew angrier the longer they drove, and every time he twisted in his seat to glare at her, she cowered more.

"New Foundations wasn't bad at first. There were other kids and all these people, and my dad kept insisting my mom would come there eventually." Insisted until the one day her uncle told her never to ask again or he'd kill her mom. She stopped talking for weeks then. "Back then it had a different name and really was a sort of commune."

"But it changed."

She guessed he knew most of the background. "Was that in your research?"

"Yeah."

She rubbed her hand over the arm banded around her stomach. Having him there, touching her, so close, settled her nerves. Made it possible to tell the story. "Things changed a few years in. My dad went from nervous and jumpy to paranoid. He was convinced the police were coming to take me away and made me practice all these drills. Learn how to shoot. My uncle seemed to encourage the mental decline and instability."

Holt placed a soft kiss on the side of her head. "Did something happen that caused the change?"

"Looking back now, I think it was gradual, or maybe he was never well. I'm not sure." She struggled to remember all he'd said, but in her young head it sounded wild and scary. Now she wondered if he suffered from delusions. It was as if he'd talked about being tracked and followed so many times that he started to believe it. "I'm not sure, but this new leader came in and the light feeling at the campground went away. I was probably twelve at the time."

That was when the fear started. Her father had told her years before about her mother dying. Showed her a clipping from the paper. The new leader made her yearn for her other life, the one before. Her father loved the guy, and soaked up every word, while her uncle hung back. It caused a rift between the brothers. One she never quite understood because she did everything to stay out of Uncle Walt's way.

"I tried to run away." Twice, but the second time resulted in her being thrown into a hole and guarded, and she had no wish to relive that in her memories. "The days got worse. People left and the guns rolled in."

"They've been up there for that long?"

She assumed that meant he had seen the storage facilities and all the weapons. "I was about fourteen when the amount of firepower started to register in my head. No one said what it was for. The adults likely knew, but I didn't."

"There's enough for a small army up there now. Weapons regular citizens shouldn't possess."

She shivered at the thought and he pulled her in tighter against his body, tucking her head under his chin. "I escaped before my fifteenth birthday. I was supposed to start learning new battle techniques. I had no idea what that meant, but I needed out. The kids rarely got to leave the camp back then."

"It's still the case. Adults can come and go with more ease."

"I hid in the back of a delivery truck. It was refrigerated and I almost froze by the time I got off the mountain and out of there." If she thought about it long enough, she could still feel the numbness in her fingers. "The older Sheriff Carver was up there all the time, so I knew not to run to him. I hitched and got far enough away where I could ask for help."

"That story makes me crazy." Holt blew out a harsh breath.

She could hear the anger in his voice but knew it wasn't aimed at her. "Why?"

"You were put in danger." His back moved as he blew out a long breath. "The police wherever you ended up didn't do anything to start an investigation at the campground?"

"I didn't contact the police. If I did, my father and uncle would find me, or at least that's what I thought." Her only goal back then had been to get out. She didn't really have the life skills to do much else, but her survival instinct kept her going. "I found a woman, who got me to another couple, who eventually got me to my aunt."

"Your mom really was dead?"

"Yes." The biggest regret of Lindsey's life was not getting out in time to let her mom know she was safe. "I went with my aunt, who taught me what I needed to know and changed my name and hid with me."

Aunt Chloe turned her life upside down for her without question. She made Lindsey promise not to go near her father ever again. When Lindsey lost her last year in a car accident, she'd lost her last ties to her extended family.

"A few years ago, my father died in a raid about a hundred miles away from here. The New Foundations folks stood up for some guy engaged in a battle with the FBI." Her aunt had delivered the news without emotion. Lindsey tried to mourn but couldn't.

Holt leaned over and kissed the side of her head. "I'm sorry."

The sweet touch sent a new spiral of warmth running through her. That and the acceptance. She didn't hear pity or disgust in his voice. Just a gentle understanding. "Great gene pool, huh?"

"Don't let your father's actions define you." Holt's hand slipped up higher, to just under her breast. "I think you're pretty amazing."

"You know I want to turn over and face you, right?"

His breath grew heavier. "Go to sleep."

He was right and she tried not to grumble about it. "Where will you be?"

"Right beside you."

She took that as a vow and let herself drift off.

ONCE SHE FINALLY fell asleep, the morning came fast. She woke up with her legs tangled with Holt's and his arms still around her. When he got up to shower, she turned and buried her face in his pillow. Smelled his scent on the sheets.

He'd left a few minutes ago to run some errands for what was supposed to be his job. He said some sort of memorial service was being planned for Grant and he had to do some things for it.

That left her alone with Shane. Not exactly a hardship, since he stood in the middle of her kitchen making her breakfast. There was no end to the talents of these Corcoran Team gentlemen.

She watched him move. He had the same easy control over his surroundings that Holt had. They both stood around six feet tall. Shane was broader and more muscular. Handsome, with his light brown hair and the scruffy start of a beard around his chin.

He had a bit of a boyish handsomeness about him. Not the dark and brooding look Holt possessed. She found Shane cute and easy to be around. Holt made her hot and jumpy and ready to replan her entire life to spend time with him.

Yeah, she was in trouble in the don't-get-attached department.

"Have a good night?" Shane glanced up at her as she took a chair at the small kitchen table. "You should see your face. It was a neutral question, I promise."

It felt more like a test. Since she guessed Shane was like Holt in that he believed in straight talk, she gave him some. "We're not sleeping together. Me and Holt, I mean."

One of Shane's eyebrows lifted. "Are you sure? Because I woke up by myself in the family room this morning."

She ignored his grin and the lift of amusement in his voice. "I meant sex."

He gave her a wink, then returned to the frying pan and cooking bacon. "Not my business."

She inhaled, enjoying the smell. Then she wondered where the groceries came from, as her idea of breakfast consisted of cereal eaten over the sink. But another more pressing question picked at her brain. "He wouldn't tell you?"

"Holt is my best friend."

Not the clearest answer, but then she guessed that might be her real answer. "I'll take that as a yes." Which raised another question. "Is he always so...bossy?"

Shane made a noise that sounded like a snort. "Absolutely."

Just as she feared. Having two of the same type under the same roof—and Shane might add a third—would make the next few days rough. "Wonderful."

He dumped the bacon on a rack and then turned back to her. A smile lit his face a second later. "Really, never play poker. You don't exactly hide your feelings well."

"Your best friend can be difficult." An understatement but not wrong.

Shane put a cup of coffee in front of her and pushed the milk container closer to her. "You should meet his sister."

Lindsey froze in the act of pouring. "I didn't know he had one."

"A baby sister. Makena." Shane got a strange look in his eyes. "She's...um."

Well, well, well. "Is the word you're looking for *hot*?"

"She's definitely that. Tall with long black hair." Shane wiped a hand over his mouth, then shook his head. "They share their Japanese mom's features and a raging case of stubbornness, which I blame on their tough career military dad."

Lindsey liked the insight into Holt and his personal life, but she got the very real sense Shane had pivoted into biographical data to keep from talking about Makena. A part of Lindsey would love to know what Holt thought about his best friend having an obvious thing for his baby sister.

Later she just might, but now she stuck with low-controversy subjects. "Sounds like a good way to grow up."

"Not really, but I'll let Holt tell you about it."

That grabbed her attention. After spilling about her past last night, she'd drifted off to sleep. Holt didn't offer up anything, but she really hadn't given him a chance. "I'm not sure he will."

Shane dumped food on her empty plate. "You don't see it?"

The aroma of eggs and bacon filled her head. She fought off the temptation to start eating before he took his share. "What?"

"How he looks at you."

Her appetite withered and she lowered her fork. "Like he wants to strangle me?"

Shane laughed. "Yeah, sometimes that, but I mean the other times."

She ran through the conversation and the things he'd said last night after the deputy left, and she came to one conclusion. "Are you matchmaking?"

"Of course not." He dug his fork into the pile

of eggs in front of him. "I'm a tough run-and-gun type."

But that twinkle in his eyes. Shane might be big, but he was also quite charming. She wondered if Makena had ever had all that attraction and cuteness aimed in her direction. The woman wouldn't stand a chance.

Shane swallowed and reached for his coffee mug. "I'm also the only one in this house sleeping alone. Just saying."

Lindsey thought about ignoring the comment but decided not to. "I don't trust many people."

"I get that, but if you're going to pick one person, Holt is the right one." Shane shoveled in another forkful of eggs and washed it down with more coffee. "And after that comment I need to go out and shoot something to get my commitment-phobic reputation back."

Definitely matchmaking. "Very reasonable."

This time he picked up bacon. "It'll give me something to do while Holt is out."

The way Shane said it clued her in. Holt had mentioned work and errands and things he needed to do, but it sounded as if Shane knew more. "Where is he?"

"The boss called him in for a one-on-one meeting."

"You mean that Connor guy who runs the

Corcoran Team, right?" She hoped but she doubted.

Shane winced. "I mean his boss at the gun-running cult. Holt is pretending to be Hank at the moment."

Her stomach dropped and a spinning started in the center of her chest. She dropped her fork and it clanked against the side of the plate. "I notice you waited until now to tell me that part."

Shane looked at her plate, then at her face. "Did the stall work?"

It only prolonged the inevitable. Now she'd worry all afternoon until Holt walked in the door again. "Let me put it this way. Do you have a gun I can borrow for some of that shooting practice?"

Shane smiled. "I'll take that as a no."

"Right."

"I like you, Lindsey Pike." Shane reached for the coffeepot. "And I promise you Holt will be fine."

She decided to believe him. It was either that or storm up to the camp, and that couldn't happen...though she might make an exception for Holt. And that scared her to death.

Chapter Nine

Simon leaned back in his chair and eyed up the man in front of him. He had the look of someone skating on the edge. Stayed in shape and scored off the charts on the shooting trials, but there was a certain something bubbling under the surface, as if he stood a step away from causing chaos. Simon liked that about him.

Without the Lindsey piece, Hank would be the ideal candidate to groom as second in command. But Lindsey's presence put that plan into serious question. Nothing new there. She had a tendency to ruin everything and everyone she touched. She would understand that soon enough.

"You've had a busy few days." Simon tapped his fingertips together as he quietly assessed and analyzed every move and reaction.

But Hank didn't give anything away. His expression never changed. His temper stayed even. When questioned about his shaky past, he insisted the day he fired on the collaterals in that

Afghanistan village he was following orders and worried for the safety of his men. Instead of being honored or winning an award he got booted. Faced charges and had to start over.

Simon knew all about starting over. It took years but he'd worked his way up at New Foundations, taking every crappy job and learning how the camp operated. When he found the training subpar, he left and acquired the skills and contacts he needed.

He returned renewed and when a position of power opened, he went for it. He removed the people in his path and made a grab for what he wanted. And when the day came to take over and spin the camp's direction, he did not hesitate.

He sensed those same qualities in Hank. Simon just had to bring them out. Mold them to what he needed.

Hank continued to stand half at attention with his arms folded in front of him and legs apart. "I'm just trying to keep my head down and do my job."

"That didn't work." When Hank frowned at that, Simon explained. "My understanding is you recently ended up in the middle of a crime scene."

"That's not exactly what happened." Hank hesitated over each word as if wondering how much he should say.

"Tell me what did." Simon knew but he wanted to test Hank's ability to tell the truth. The man bucked authority since authority had jerked him around, but Simon demanded full obedience. It was one of the things missing from his predecessor's regime. The first thing Simon did after he cleaned out the members who would slow them down and try to tinker with his vision.

"My friend owns the property where Grant's body was found," Hank said.

A sanitized version. Simon appreciated that Hank could offer one, but he needed more. Mostly, he needed Hank to know all of his moves were being watched and accept it. "Lindsey Pike."

"Do you know her?"

"Of her." An understatement, but the answer worked for now and Simon was not ready to explain. But soon. "The deputy sheriff has been asking questions about her and Grant."

Hank leaned in. A subtle move but noticeable if you watched closely, and Simon did. A potentially dangerous thing since jealousy and ridiculous talk of love had led to the downfall of more than one man.

"What do you mean?" Hank asked.

"Grant had a crush on Lindsey." Simon repeated the made-up tale. "He came over and you two kicked him off the property. Not to state the obvious issue but now he's dead. Even ignoring New Foundations' stated preference for its members not to draw attention, the timing is not ideal."

Hank returned to his expressionless stance, looking both rigid and disinterested. "You think I'm involved."

Simon dodged that question more to test Hank's reaction than anything else. "Surely, you can see where law enforcement would draw some conclusions."

"They're wrong."

The guy stayed solid. Didn't shake. Good to know. "I'm sure, but still we need to play this the right way."

"I don't know what you mean."

"Sit down." Simon gestured to the seat in front of him and waited until Hank, like the good soldier he was, obeyed. "You should come back to the bunkhouse. For now."

"I would prefer to stay with her." Before Simon could respond, Hank continued. "I have a friend in town and he's staying with me at Lindsey's house, as well. It would be awkward for him to be there while I'm not. She barely knows him."

Unexpected news. Simon hadn't planned ahead for another new player in town. Nothing in Hank's file pointed to him even having friends. "I had the impression after your military issues your support system disappeared."

"All but this guy. He was there and tried to testify for me." Hank remained as blank as ever. "I've actually been thinking about introducing him to you and the idea of the camp. He would appreciate what we do here."

Simon didn't care for the turn in the conversation. He'd learned from his short time in charge to be aware of tone and subtext. "Which is what? What do you think we do here?"

"Live our lives without hassles. No government interference. No rules except the ones agreed to long ago." Something close to a smile formed on Hank's mouth. "That's why I came here and why I stayed."

"And no one here is subjected to the government's idea of criminal charges." Simon believed in handling issues in-house, which explained Grant's current state.

"Exactly. I've had enough of those."

Simon liked that Hank didn't try to deny or explain. Not that he could do the former. They'd talked about his past in the very first interview. "That's why I think you should be a little careful with Ms. Pike."

"Is that a warning?" Hank asked in a voice suddenly filled with venom.

Simon matched Hank's attitude with some of his own. "Does it need to be?"

"I don't intend to stop seeing her."

Interesting. Simon still couldn't tell if that insistence made Hank an ally or an enemy, but it did set off an alarm that Simon would not ignore. "Of course not, but I am considering increasing your duties here. Moving you into Grant's position and providing you with more extensive training."

"I would appreciate that."

Of course he would. Anyone would, especially the type who came to the camp. Simon understood the need of men to belong and feel as if they were accomplishing something.

Up until now they'd been working behind the scenes. Fighting the government by supplying weapons to a militia here and providing men on the ground there against the ATF. For the next step to work, the promise of instability and the reorganization, New Foundations needed to move into the leadership role and not just be the might behind the fight.

Leading sometimes meant destroying and rebuilding. It was a general principle most people forgot these days. They threw money and people on the same problem over and over again. He would not make that mistake.

"The position requires, at times, taking on some difficult tasks," Simon said, laying the groundwork.

Hank nodded. "I'm fine with that."

"If Ms. Pike had something to do with Grant's death, your loyalties could be tested."

A stark silence pounded through the room. The clock on the edge of his desk ticked and the springs on his chair let out a slight squeak as he rocked back and forth.

It took a full minute for Hank to speak again. "If she did it, I'll drag her up here myself to atone for her crimes."

Right answer. "I knew I could count on you."

HOLT BARELY MADE it in the door before he heard Lindsey's heavy sigh.

She started walking toward him then jogged. She hit his chest with her arms wrapped around his neck. "You're home."

The relationship bounced around from on-the-verge-of-sex to trying to maintain control. After holding her last night, smelling her hair and touching her skin, Holt doubted he could go back to playing indifferent, so he didn't try.

His arms tightened around her and he placed a quick kiss on her lips. "I should leave more often."

Shane cleared his throat. Since he practically

stood on top of them, it was hard to miss. "I was thinking the same thing."

A red flush stained Lindsey's cheeks and she tried to step back. "Sorry."

Holt didn't let her get far. He hated the idea of her being embarrassed or using the reaction this time as an excuse not to show him affection next time. He telegraphed all of that in a kiss, this one slower and a bit more lingering, before he let her go. "Don't be."

She stood there, fidgeting as she rubbed her hands together. "I just thought you could be in trouble. That—"

"It's okay." And it was...for now. He'd played the role of Hank without slipping even though he'd had to fight off the urge to smash a fist into Simon Falls's face the entire time they talked in his office.

"Is it?"

Fear. He got that from her voice and the relief in her eyes when he walked in. She worried for him and he did not hate the sensation of having someone care about him. "True, Simon Falls threatened. He worked that in along with trying to plant the seed you killed Grant."

She went from nervous to ticked off in two seconds. It was an amazing thing to see. She drew up, her shoulders stiffening, and a new determination washed over her. "What?"

Yeah, he knew that would get her attention. "After that, Simon moved on to offering me Grant's job...sort of."

Shane nodded. "So, your typical business meeting."

As if Holt knew. "Don't ask me. I've never had one."

"Go back." Lindsey stepped between them with a hand on Holt's chest and another hovering in the air in front of Shane. "He's blaming me?"

"He and Deputy Carver." That was the interesting part for Holt. Simon made sure to mention law enforcement, which made little sense for a man like him. Sure, he probably had to walk a fine line, but if he really did want to start his own militia, cozying up to the sheriff seemed like an odd course.

Shane shot her an I-told-you-so smirk. "Remember my comment about the setup? Here you go. These are the building blocks."

"This is sick." She touched a hand to her head.

Holt lowered it again so he could see her face. The fact he kept holding on meant nothing. "What do you know about Falls?"

"I've never seen or met him. He never leaves the campground. I once tried to have someone smuggle out a photo but it didn't work." She shrugged, clearly frustrated by the walls she kept hitting. "All my research points to a guy who appeared on the scene out of nowhere and moved into the leadership role when the person above him died."

That all sounded familiar. "Us, too. This Falls character didn't exist before a few years ago."

"Right when the accident that wasn't occurred," Shane mumbled.

Her gaze shot to him. "What?"

Holt decided it was best she knew what they knew. "We've reviewed the record and think someone tampered with the guy's car."

"You mean Simon Falls." She looked from one man to the other. "He killed the guy in power and took over."

"Simon did benefit from the death." Holt didn't have the proof. He also didn't have a doubt that was what happened, but he'd like some verification about Simon from people who lived there. "Do you have files on other people up there?"

"Yes." Lindsey launched right into offering help. Gone was the stalling and backtracking from when they first met. "I'd start with Todd."

"Lindsey, we need to talk to the people who got out. The intel we have doesn't show anyone escaping," Shane explained.

For the first time since they'd started talking about the camp she smiled. "You don't have the intel because I'm good."

"You made that happen? You engineered the escapes?" Shane asked, clearly impressed.

"I get them out. New Foundations lies in order to keep its 'no one ever wants to leave us' motto clean, but there are people who have escaped, those I've helped and probably more who got out before I stepped up."

If he hadn't been attracted to her before then that explanation would have done it. Holt admired her and genuinely liked her. He was also determined to protect her, and that meant digging into her private life and all of her accomplishments in uncomfortable ways. "You can get us a meeting?"

She bit her bottom lip but then nodded. "Yes."

"That's trusting." He liked it.

"Are you telling me you can't be trusted?" The words sounded tough but she said it in a joking voice.

"I'm telling you I'm the one man you need to believe in." And he wasn't kidding. He meant it to his soul.

She nodded. "Done."

WHILE LINDSEY GATHERED her intel and files and all the material she kept in coded folders that no one could read because they didn't make sense as written, Holt stepped outside. The weather had turned and a warm air blew over the porch.

He heard a noise but didn't have to turn around to check it out. He'd known Shane long enough to know he'd follow.

Shane took up the position next to Holt and stared out over the lawn. "So…"

That was just about as much as Holt wanted to hear. "Stop talking."

"Not going to happen." Shane turned and leaned against the post. The move put him face-to-face with Holt. "You still saying she's just a job?"

Holt wanted to say yes, but he couldn't force the word out. "No."

"That's progress."

He didn't even know how to explain it. He'd known her for a short time, but he'd been watching her for longer. Her looks knocked him flat, but there was something about her strength that reeled him in. Now that he had a window into her past and all the chances she'd taken, he couldn't help being in awe of her.

This was not a woman who ran or withered. She'd meet him head-on, not take his grumpiness personally. Question was whether she'd welcome him into her bed again. "She's…special."

"Agreed." Shane held up a hand as soon as he said the word. "Don't look at me like that. I mean for you. I like you two together."

The anger welling up inside Holt died back

down. Shane wasn't blind and Holt understood that, but Shane didn't quite get this point. "We're not."

"You gave up the couch last night. I know because I woke up and took it."

Yeah, there was no way to dodge that fact, so Holt didn't try. "She was upset."

Shane leaned his head back against the railing. "You are not really going to use that excuse for wanting her, are you?"

"I don't deny it." Holt had to give in. Blaming Lindsey amounted to being a coward on this score.

Truth was he'd walked into that room, knocked on that door, because he'd heard the faint tap of footsteps. He only picked up on that because he was attuned to everything about her and looking for any excuse to get her to open that door.

"You *can't* deny." Shane pointed at Holt's head. "It's obvious in the way you look at her and watch her move around the room."

That sounded kind of pathetic. Holt had seen Cam fall under Julia's spell. Had heard all about the others treading water as they met these certain women. Like her or not, want to sleep with her or not, Holt still didn't want to get sucked into that kind of mess.

"It's an attraction." That wasn't a lie, so he went with it.

"No, man. It's more than that."

Holt refused to bend on this. "I am not Cam or the other guys. I'm not looking to get all tripped up by a woman."

But the more he said it, the less he believed it. He tried to work up his usual horror at the idea of being trapped and tied to one woman. Not that he slept around or liked to lead women on. He absolutely didn't. He lived by one simple creed when it came to women—treat them how he would want his sister treated. That meant with respect and honesty.

He always started off by making the parameters clear. Fun and nothing more. He tried to remember if he'd delivered that speech to Lindsey. They'd been racing on fast forward since they met. There had barely been room for any sort of understanding...and he couldn't bring himself to suggest whatever he had with her would be fleeting at best.

The woman was tying him up in knots and he couldn't get free. Now he had to figure out if he even wanted to.

"One thing?" Shane's tone suggested this could be a kick-to-the-gut type of thing.

Holt knew he should say no. Should walk away. Maybe get in the truck and go for a drive to clear his head. "What?"

"Tonight when you go into her room—and

you will, so don't deny it—maybe test and see how deep that attraction goes."

Holt's mind zipped to the night and Lindsey in those near-see-through pajamas and his brain shut down. "You're giving me love-life advice?"

"I'm trying to save you from running around in circles like Cam just did."

Holt feared it might be too late. "That's not something I would do."

"Right." Shane pushed off from the railing. "You keep thinking that."

Chapter Ten

Late that afternoon Holt's truck pulled into the driveway in front of what looked like an old barn. The inside had been converted. A brother and sister lived in there, watching over the camp from afar and feeding information to Lindsey whenever possible.

She'd helped them get out, but truth was they were about to run away from the place on their own. From time to time, she'd stumbled onto Kurt Noonan buying maps and stealing tips from the café she worked in. It had taken Lindsey forever to build up enough trust to move in and make contact. But she had and now Kurt and Kelly were out.

That's why Lindsey liked the café. Her aunt had left her with enough to be comfortable with her conservative money-spending lifestyle, but Lindsey needed to fit in and be able to gather intel, and working part-time at the café proved to be the perfect place for that.

She shut the truck door and came around to the front to stand next to Holt. Together they stared at the peeling red paint and what deceptively looked like a door half off its hinges. Grass grew wild and the tree branches inched closer to the house.

No one would ever guess about the technology setup in there. That would teach Simon Falls to educate kids on computer warfare.

"Where's Shane?" she asked, thinking a third hand with a gun would not be a terrible idea.

Kurt and Kelly feared for their safety. Knowing two bodyguards stood watch might put them at ease.

"Doing a full-scale search of Roger's cabin with Cam. They have some equipment to detect explosives and are going to plot out the safe places to move around on the property."

The words fell flat inside her. "You mean they're over there searching for his body."

One of Holt's eyebrows lifted. "Did I say that?"

He could skip the defensiveness, because she got it. From the first time she saw that blood pool, she'd known. This was not a case of Roger faking his death. This time he was gone. She could feel it to her bones. "Didn't have to."

With Grant dead and her the lead suspect for some reason, Holt claimed reporting Roger missing would only shine the spotlight brighter on her. The decision not to run to Frank Jr. with this, too, eased some of the anxiety pinging around inside her.

She followed Holt's gaze. Watched him do his usual scan of the area. He stood always ready to protect and defend. It was one of the many things she liked about him.

He frowned at her. "I thought you told them we were coming."

As much as he seemed to enjoy the frowning thing, it annoyed her. She filed that away for later because she would tell him. "I did."

Holt leaned against the front of the truck. "Looks like no one's home."

"Always does." Lindsey was prepared to be worried about a lot right now but not this one thing. "That's part of the subterfuge."

"They're certain that someone from New Foundations is going to track them down and, what, drag them back?" The tone made the idea sound far-fetched. As if Simon Falls had better things to do with his time.

Lindsey knew better. "Kill them. The stockpile of weapons have some people up there twitchy, and that was before the newest round that you say is so dangerous was delivered."

"It's hard-core lethal."

That was the part Lindsey couldn't understand. Never did. They had the weapons and the ability to fire them. What then? Unless the guy planned to do battle with the next town over, the arsenal didn't make sense.

She joined him in leaning. Felt the heat of the engine seep through her clothes. "Is Simon Falls planning on blowing up the town of Justice?"

"I wish I knew. If someone is in on it, they're keeping it quiet."

That wasn't even a little hard to believe. "People up there thrive on secrets."

"True." He stood up and held out a warning hand to her. "Stay here."

As far as exits went, that was a good one. But it would not get him anywhere. They stood twenty feet away from the front door, and Lindsey doubted the Noonans would let them get more than a few inches closer without unleashing something. "They won't let you in."

"I get that, but I need to know it's safe for you to come with me." Holt kept walking, watching her but throwing glances in the direction of the building's front door.

When he breached what she knew Kurt considered to be the final perimeter and nothing happened, something twisted inside her. She jumped away from the car. "Holt, wait."

He immediately stopped. Didn't question her warning, just obeyed. "What is it?"

"Something."

He gestured toward the truck with a flick of his chin as he hit a button on his watch. "Get back in."

"Too late." She didn't know, but she sensed that to be true. It was as if a huge ticking clock swung over her head and she could hear the ripping sound as it tore away, ready to crush her.

"Do not move." He held a hand out to her as if that would stop her.

She might listen, but he still didn't understand the people he was dealing with here. Kurt and Kelly were people with nothing left to lose because they'd lost everything, including the parents still inside whom they hadn't seen in two years. "I could be wrong and if I am they won't let you in."

He frowned at her. "Yes, they will."

She was all for confidence and a healthy shot of ego, but this was about safety. The idea of seeing him go down and watching the blood run out of his body nearly dropped her to her knees.

She had the sudden need to heave but bit it back. "They are trained, Holt. They will shoot you without question and not care how much I scream for them to stop. They might only be in their early twenties, but they spent most of their teen years being indoctrinated into a certain way of dealing with outsiders."

Something got through, because his demeanor changed and resignation set in. "Fine."

She was at his side a few steps later. Today she held one of Shane's backup guns. It fit her hand and she'd practiced with it a few times, but she missed her own. The idea of it showing up somewhere connected to a crime scene sent a chill through her.

She still remembered racing into the house after Shane's dire warning that it would be gone. The safe in her nightstand had been broken into. The gun gone.

But that was days ago. Now she ignored the fear and the frustration and focused on the adrenaline. It pumped through her, sending her heart racing in a wild beat.

The closer they got to the door, the more the dread settled in. She instinctively knew something had happened. If they walked into another crime scene, complete with blood, she might just lose it for the first time in her life.

Holt turned before getting to the front door. He took them around the right side of the building. He looked up and around the walls, his gaze never stopping as they closed in.

She wanted to ask about the plan, but she wasn't sure there was one. But he had a destination in mind. Maybe he hoped to peek in a window, but that was not going to happen. The windows consisted of long slits, smaller than the size of a person and set up high. The Noonans had thought about everything when they converted this place.

As they slid along the side, Lindsey heard something. Faint and almost undecipherable. A noise, possibly the whistle of the breeze through the trees surrounding the building. Whatever it was. Holt must have picked it up, too, because he stopped. Froze and signaled for her to hold up.

Then she heard it again. An animal's cry maybe? So soft. So odd.

Holt watched each step as he started moving again. The pebbles crunched under their feet, but he somehow limited the noise.

By the time they got to the back corner of the building, her nerves buzzed. The quiet had her jumping and glancing around. She couldn't shake the sensation she was being watched. Stalked.

With his back to the wall, Holt looked around the corner. He shifted and then shifted back without making a sound. He stared at her and widened his eyes. She knew it was some sort of signal, but she didn't know for what. That was enough to keep her quiet and standing there at the ready.

Holt looked again. This time longer. He must have seen something, and curiosity had her turning to try to look over his shoulder. No sooner had her front touched his back than she heard the noise. This one clear.

The crunch of stones had her turning back to where they just came from. The man appeared out of thin air. One second she heard the footsteps and the next a guy was almost on top of her. Not Kurt or Kelly or anyone else she knew. A stranger with a feral grin and a shiny gun.

He slammed into her side, sending them both sprawling to the ground. Her gun bounced out of her hand as she made a grab for Holt. She felt only air as her body flew. She landed with a hard thud on the ground. She expected the attacker to fall on top of her, pin her down, but nothing happened.

When she opened her eyes again, she saw Holt grab the guy. The men grunted and thuds rang out as they each landed punches. In form and fighting style they appeared evenly matched.

The attacker smashed Holt's body into the wall, and the wood cracked beneath him. Then Holt landed a knee to the stomach.

They fell and rolled. The world whipped around her as a blur of men and dark clothes passed in slow motion in front of her. She patted the ground and scanned the grass for her gun. If she could grab the weapon and separate one man from the other, at least in her mind, she might be able to get off a shot.

As she watched, the attacker gained the advantage. After a series of punches to Holt's side, the attacker threw him on the ground and straddled him. Slipped a knife out of a holder by his ankle and held it up over Holt.

Lindsey scrambled to find the weapon—any weapon. She needed to punch and kick. She'd made it to her knees, ready to jump on the guy and at least buy Holt time, when she saw a flash. Holt, looking defeated a second ago, lifted an arm. Got the gun between him and the attacker and fired.

The shot rang out. The attacker froze. The knife dropped as his hand went to his stomach. Red slipped through his fingers, and his eyes rolled back. Holt didn't wait for him to fall. He shoved the man to the side and rolled away.

Lindsey unfroze from her spot and took off on her knees. She crawled over to Holt's sprawled body. He had to be in pain and possibly on the verge of unconsciousness.

"Holt?" He said something in response, but she didn't hear it. She leaned in closer. "What are you saying?"

His eyes popped open, clear and filled with anger. "We need to find the Noonans."

He jackknifed into a sitting position. The

move, so quick and sudden, scared her. She waited for him to fall over. Instead, he jumped to his feet.

Then it hit her. The defensive position and all those groans as the attacker landed punches... all fake. "Are you hurt at all?"

"No, but the guy could hit."

Holt acted as though getting pummeled was no big deal. The other man had rammed his fist in Holt's side over and over. Any other man would have fallen down in defeat. Not Holt. He created a ruse and lured the guy in. Lindsey looked over at the attacker's still form and decided the right way to say it was that Holt lured him in and then killed him.

Without missing a beat, Holt checked the attacker for a pulse, then pocketed his weapon. Next he scooped up her gun and handed it to her. She stumbled around in a stupor. She hadn't even been able to get off her knees.

He held a hand down to her. "Let's go."

She took it and got up. Rounding the corner, she saw what he'd been staring at. The tall grass around the back of the house had been trampled down for a long stretch. The path led away from the building and toward a second, much smaller one, half a football field's length away.

Ducking down, Holt took off. He followed the path, walking beside it. She followed, keeping low. Her footing faltered when she glanced down at the crushed grass and saw blood. Not a tiny trickle. This was enough to leave a long smear.

Panic whirred to life inside her. Her emotions had been bouncing from relief to fear, teetering one minute to the next. Now they stayed locked on blinding fear.

Her fingers tapped against Holt's back to let him know she was there. He treated her to a short nod and kept going, which was exactly what she wanted. The danger hadn't lapsed for the Noonans, people she considered both rescues and friends of a sort. Kindred spirits at least.

The storage shed sat away from the house. They kept everything in there from tissues to food. The shed housed their end-of-the-world supplies. They'd been so indoctrinated by Simon Falls that they couldn't shake the hoarding tendency loose.

Holt looked around with an expression filled with scorn. She thought he might circle the shed looking for windows and thought to warn him. She didn't have time. He lifted his leg and kicked the door in.

The wood shattered and the lock broke open with a crack. The door bounced, but Holt caught it with his shoulder. Going in first, he moved and hustled…then stopped.

Dread and sadness crashed over her in waves. "What is it?"

Holt didn't stop to answer. He flew across the room to where Kelly was tied to a chair. He felt for a pulse and cut her free. With gentle hands, he laid her down against the floor.

Lindsey almost missed it all because she was busy hovering over Kurt's lifeless form. He lay doubled over, almost in the fetal position. She checked for a pulse and couldn't find one. Convinced her emergency skills were on the fritz, she looked to Holt.

He was already moving. He slid in beside her and felt for a pulse. Then tried again. He turned Kurt over and blood drained from the injury in his shoulder, washing over Holt's hands to the floor.

He glanced up at her. "We need an ambulance, and fast. I don't know what directions to give, so you'll have to."

As if she could remember at that moment. "Right."

"Here's my phone. Press number seven and say medical transport." He shook the phone. "Not 9-1-1 or anything else. Only number seven."

With her mind turned to mush, she struggled to understand his message. There were things in the house the police couldn't see. A treasure trove of intel on New Foundations ferreted out online. "But what about—"

"Connor will handle the rest."

She had no idea what that meant. Her brain raced to catch up but failed. All she could do was stare at him.

In the beat of hesitation, Holt grabbed her arm. Not hard but enough to kick her out of her stupor. "Now, Lindsey."

"Right." She reached for the cell and punched it in.

His hand slipped farther down her arm. "I get the worries, but you need to trust me on this."

She looked at Kelly, then Kurt. They'd been beaten and shot. Even now bruises formed. Kurt took the brunt, but Kelly had not been spared either. The attacker clearly didn't care that she was a young woman, which confirmed everything Lindsey already knew about the group.

"Number seven, then Deputy Carver." Holt nodded at her after issuing the order.

"Why him?"

"As hard as it's going to be, it's time to start flushing Falls out." Holt's expression grew even darker. "Before he attacks anyone else."

This time she didn't disagree or even blink. She just followed the instructions and hoped Holt knew what he was talking about. She wasn't one to trust and she was placing a lot in him and this Connor person she'd never even met.

By the time the ambulance arrived and the victims were loaded, she'd become convinced everything she knew and everything she cared about was about to blow up.

Holt stepped up beside her as the second ambulance took off. "You okay?"

"No." She couldn't even travel to the hospital with the Noonans. Not really.

Deputy Carver had acted exactly as Holt predicted. The deputy clearly assumed the Noonans had been loaded into normal medical transport. After all, the ambulance looked legitimate. But no. Holt arranged for something else.

He had ambulances on his payroll, or Corcoran's, that would take the couple somewhere safe. That meant she'd hear any new information relayed through Holt. While she hated losing control, under the current circumstances, she needed the help.

She rubbed her hands over her arms, but what she really wanted was him holding her. "I need to go home and pretend this day never happened."

He nodded without looking at her. "I agree."

That was a surprise. "No speech about how everything is going to be okay."

"I'll give that once I find the missing body."

The comment hit her like one more body blow. "What?"

"The attacker I shot? Gone."

She heard his anger, but the words got muffled. She turned them over in her head, trying to make sense of them. "Not possible."

"Looks like whatever militia Simon Falls is building is coming after us." Holt finally looked at her. "Good news is I like our chances."

That made one of them.

Chapter Eleven

Simon stood with Deputy Carver near the main gate of New Foundations. A high fence outlined a portion of the hundreds of acres owned by them. The rest was set off with a shorter electrified fence, along with motion sensors and warning signs that promised a bullet for trespassing.

Guards watched the front, and people mingled inside the walls. No one knew about the danger lurking just outside. They'd heard about Grant and assumed a vagrant shot him. For now, Simon was content to let that story stand to all but the elite staff members who answered only to him and shared his vision.

Simon had listened to Frank Jr. talk about the attacks on a couple he described as random. Heard all about Lindsey and Hank being found there with the Noonans.

The job of framing Lindsey Pike just got easier and easier.

Simon moved in for the kill. "You no longer have a choice but to do something about her."

"I don't have any forensic evidence linking Lindsey to any crime." The deputy waved to a couple walking nearby. They didn't respond with anything other than by looking away. "I think it's more likely that Hank guy. He comes to Justice and people start dying."

"Interesting theory, but he's been up here with us." And getting Hank arrested didn't serve any real purpose for Simon. If anything, finding another man with those skills and that temperament would take forever. So, no, he'd need to remain free. "Lindsey is the one you need to bring in."

"Possibly."

Simon decided to let it lie there. For now. He would push later. Bring up some information Frank Jr. either didn't know or did a good job of hiding. Simon would be more impressed if the case were the latter, but he suspected the former.

Buying his father off had been easy. A beloved sheriff with a small pension and a big heart condition. Simon stuck to Frank Sr.'s practical side and got a mountain of assistance in return. No interference at the camp and a free flow of information.

Now it was Frank Jr.'s turn, though he didn't seem to realize it yet. But soon he would.

"What's the plan now?" Simon asked, trying to keep the disgust out of his voice.

"Collect more evidence."

A response Simon couldn't control, which made it his least favorite option. "What can I do for you?"

"I need everything you have on Hank."

Now Simon had a problem. He wanted to make a scene and bring the deputy in line right now, but there were too many people around. And some things needed to be handled in privacy. That gave Frank Jr. a reprieve for now. "I'll send it over."

"Appreciate it." The deputy nodded, then walked away. Right past the guard and through the gate. Out into a world where he could do nothing but cause trouble.

Todd appeared at Simon's side. He stood there but wisely did not say a word.

Simon wanted to break the man in two.

"Maybe you would like to tell me why you suddenly can't handle a simple job." Simon smiled and waved at the people he saw, but inside he seethed.

"Hank and Lindsey came in a beat too early." Todd scanned the area, never showing any outward sign of distress or blowback from what he had done. "Jeb panicked."

"And now he's dead." That counted two men

dead. Simon hated losing anyone. The training needed to bring people up through the ranks proved daunting, but Simon had bigger concerns at the moment. "Jeb is a man who could trace back to me, who definitely traces back to New Foundations. It's only by pure luck he'd been doing survival training and hadn't met Hank."

"I took care of him." Todd cleared his throat and lowered his voice. "No one will find the body."

Simon wanted to argue about forensic evidence, but he let it drop. "I have a new job for you. This is your last chance to prove to me you can handle it."

"Yes, sir."

"Figure out how to take the deputy's attention off Hank." Simon thought about all he had planned for Lindsey and how none of that would happen if she left town in a panic. "And make it quick."

LINDSEY SLAMMED EVERY cabinet door in the kitchen. Holt knew because he stood right there listening to the drum show. They waited for Shane to return with news. Holt toyed with the idea of diverting her attention, but now, when her nerves rode the edge, was not the time for more kissing. Which was a damn shame.

Just when he thought he couldn't take the

noise for one more second, Shane walked in. He hit the alarm code before it started screaming, then came into the kitchen.

Lindsey spun around. "Well?"

"Kelly is in stable condition." He stopped there.

Holt knew that was a bad sign. If Shane had good news he'd spill it, especially if he noticed the hope on Lindsey's face, which seemed hard to miss. But they needed everything out in the open, so Holt asked, "Kurt?"

"He didn't make it."

Lindsey sat down hard on the kitchen chair. Her mouth opened and her eyes filled. Her pain vibrated out of her and took over the entire room.

Holt wanted to go to her, and he would, but he needed to know where they were first. "Give me the full report."

Shane didn't need further coaxing. He launched right into it, even though his usually lighter tone had disappeared. "Cam and Connor are making arrangements to get Kelly to safety once she can travel."

Holt waited for Lindsey to pipe up. To say anything. Instead she just sat there, almost in a daze of sadness. With flat eyes and a pale face, she sat motionless. All the life and energy that usually buzzed around her had disappeared.

He reached over and grabbed the list Lindsey

had compiled while they waited. "She saved six others. Most relocated outside of Oregon."

"I contacted them." Lindsey's voice cut through the quiet, sounding more mechanical than human.

As each minute passed he worried more about her and how she would cope. Losing Kurt, losing anyone she'd helped, would be a huge blow. Most people would shrivel and stop functioning. He hoped she would spin out of it.

"Connor helped." Holt could still hear Connor's calm voice as he worked with Lindsey to reassure everyone.

Shane nodded. "I just talked with him. He's dispatching Joel and a few others to get these people, relocate them and watch over them until we know what's going on."

The news brought relief. The tightening in Holt's chest finally eased.

"But Kurt is still dead and Roger is missing." Lindsey stood up. Went to the refrigerator and opened the door. Just stood there doing nothing as the cold air escaped.

"We're going to get these guys," Holt said, vowing to do just that.

She glanced at him over his shoulder. "After how many more people die?"

"Hopefully none." And Holt meant that. He couldn't promise everything would run smoothly and no one would get hurt, so he didn't try. But he could make a vow. One to protect and defend.

She shut the refrigerator door. "I'm going to bed."

That was all she said and then she walked out of the room. Down the hall. Holt waited to hear the soft click behind her.

Before he could say anything, Shane jumped in. "She's having a rough time."

"This sucks for her." People dead at her feet and attackers behind every door. It was too much for him, and he played this game every single day at work.

"Tonight when you go in there to help her sleep, throw everything at her to reassure her."

Holt wasn't even sure what tools he could bring to that. "Maybe she needs a break. Some alone time."

Shane shook his head. "If you think that, you still aren't getting it."

Holt had no idea what that meant, but he was a hundred percent sure Shane was right. "Any chance you're going to be out of the house tonight?"

A grin spread across Shane's mouth. "That's more like it. Give me ten minutes and I'll disappear. Check the grounds and watch from a distance so you won't need to guard your back."

"You have five minutes."

Chapter Twelve

Lindsey wasn't in the mood to be coddled or placated. She wasn't a fragile doll, but she wasn't heartless either. She knew how a person could wither without affection and what it did to everything from your self-esteem to your outlook on life.

Someone she'd helped and nurtured and groomed to fit better into the real world was gone. At twenty-two. It amounted to a sick and horrible waste. She had no idea how Kelly would recover when the only support she'd ever had was her brother, now dead.

And then there was Roger…and Grant, whom she didn't know but who should still be mourned. The guy outside the Noonans' house. The bodies kept piling up until her insides shook with fear.

She sat on her bed, then stood up. When the nerves in her hands began to tremble, she rubbed her palms together. Was it really just a week ago when she was happy to lock and relock and check and triple-check her doors each night?

That made her feel safe. Now she knew how naive that all was.

"Lindsey?"

She didn't hear a knock or the door. Nothing but Holt's deep voice as it filled her room and moved through her head. "Do you need something?"

He stepped inside and closed the door behind him. "You."

She couldn't have heard that right. All the adrenaline and crackling of her nerves had her brain misfiring. She looked up and tried to read his expression but couldn't. "What did you just say?"

"Nothing."

"I don't think that's true."

His hand went back to the doorknob. "I can leave."

"No." She practically shouted the denial.

"Okay." He stepped farther into the room. Kept coming until he got to the bed. Then he sat down beside her.

The mattress dipped from his weight, and her body slid into his. "I can't seem to calm my nerves. I feel like I'm six seconds from flying apart."

His palm slipped over her thigh. "It's aftermath."

"It's pretty awful." She thought that qualified

as the understatement of the century. "Do you always feel like this?"

"Just sometimes." He slid his hand over hers and their fingers entwined. "Your nerve endings are on fire. The danger and fear, the sadness and pain. It's all mixing and getting jammed up inside you."

"How do I get rid of it?" She flipped his hand over and studied his palm. Such a strong hand. Long fingers and the calluses of a man who engaged in physical labor on a regular basis.

"Different things work for different people." His thumb rubbed against the back of her hand. Slow, lazy circles that soothed her even as her insides continued to churn.

Bold had worked for her once before. She tried it again. "Any chance kissing does the trick?"

He froze for a second before resuming the intoxicating touching. "I am trying very hard not to be a jerk here."

She'd never thought of him that way. Stubborn, yes. The man could give classes in that. "You're not."

"Are you sure? Because it feels like I'm about to cross the boundary."

He'd lost her. "What do you mean?"

He shook his head, and his voice dipped even lower. "You're upset and I don't want to take advantage."

Wow, was he misreading the situation! The worry was sweet but misplaced. If anything, her mind wandered in the other direction. She'd made it clear she was interested. Even made a not-so-subtle offer in bed last night. He ignored it all.

She'd begun to think he could fight back his feelings for her without trouble, which was not the most flattering idea in the world. Also made her crazed with a mix of disappointment and sadness.

She knew that was ridiculous now. Energy whirled around him, but he kept it in check. He was so set on doing his job that he put being a man with needs aside. She wanted him to let loose. To trust her enough to take a chance.

But he needed to say it. She could not be alone in taking the risk. "Do you want me?"

"Since the first time I saw you in the café. Not a question and don't ever doubt it." There was no hesitation in his words or in his smile. "The way you looked and the way you carried yourself. The mix of strength and hotness had me forgetting about the assignment, and for the record, that never happens."

She wasn't sure what to say, so she went with the obvious. "Wow."

"You poured my coffee in the café and I was

lost. And watching you walk?" He whistled. "Lost my mind."

For some reason the idea of that made her laugh. "I'm pretty good with coffee."

"I'd say."

She jumped right to the part that mattered. To the words spinning in her head that she was so desperate to say. "I want you, too."

He stared at her, with his gaze searching her face. His eyes softened and that sweet smile continued to play on his lips. "You sure?"

"Yes."

He mumbled something about timing. "Maybe we should wait until—"

Absolutely not. "What? Bodies stop dropping? I'm not sure when that will be."

He shifted a little, turned to face her head-on. "We're going to get this figured out and keep you safe."

With every sentence they emotionally moved further apart. He didn't get her concerns or where her mind had gone. "I'm not worried about me right now. I'm sick about what happened, but every second you sit here a new feeling inches its way in."

"Describe it."

The words wouldn't come. She couldn't think of one big enough. "Desire. I don't know what else you'd call it."

"Maybe I should just kiss you and we'll work on definitions later."

About time. "Yes."

She expected him to lean over and start with a gentle kiss. Not Holt. He lifted her, turned her. She moved through the air and when she landed she straddled his lap with a knee on either side of his hips.

Before she could catch her breath and before the room stopped spinning, his mouth covered hers. It was a kiss filled with hunger. A promise of the night to come. Her vision blurred and her fingers dug into his shoulders through his T-shirt. She held on as the world whipped around them.

His lips crossed over hers, coaxing and exploring. He'd deepen the kiss until her breathing kicked up and her heartbeat raced; then he'd gentle it. Every move and shift had her mentally begging for more. And when his mouth kissed in a trail down her neck, then up to that small dip at the base of her ear, her control evaporated.

Forget being smart. Forget the danger and the worries. She wanted this—him—right now. Just the two of them. Not about rescue or protection. About attraction flipping around wildly and out of control. About a welling inside her and a thirst that needed to be quenched.

The room tilted as his arm wrapped tighter

around her and his palm balanced against her lower back. One minute she was on his lap, kissing as she felt his body reacting to her closeness. The next, her back hit the mattress and a hundred eighty pounds of pure hot male moved over her.

She welcomed his weight. From this position she could trace those pronounced cheekbones and see the bits of brown in those near-black eyes.

Her fingertips traveled over his shoulders. When she couldn't take even the small barrier of his clothes between them one more second, she reached down and stripped the tee off him. Up his torso and gone. Then her hands touched skin. She almost sighed.

Her fingers skimmed old scars. Battle wounds. She learned every angle and line of his chest and back, and he didn't do anything to stop her. His groan cheered her on. And when her hands came to rest on the elastic waist of his boxers, he lifted his hips, as if urging her to go on.

She'd just decided to dive in when she felt his hands move. Fingers slipped up her waist, under her top. The flimsy cotton proved no match for his strong hands. He had the material bunched up around her neck and then off.

Then his mouth was on her. Licking and kissing. One breast, then the other. Every nerve ending snapped to life. With each pass of his tongue, her hips lifted higher off the mattress to flatten against his erection. He had her thrashing on the bed, her head shifting side to side.

The mix of his mouth and his hands set her whole body on fire. When his hand dipped into her pajama shorts, past her underwear to settle on her heat, she nearly jumped. He was an expert at everything, and this proved to be no exception.

He caressed and her legs tightened against his hips. She wanted him touching her, inside her. She slid her hand down the front of his briefs and cupped his erection. Her fingers moved over him, testing his length, and he groaned in response.

When he lifted off her, she grabbed for his arm, trying to pull him back. "Holt?"

"Condom." He didn't go far. Just to the dresser near the door.

She saw him pick something up. As he got closer, she recognized the packet. "You had it in my room?"

"In my hand when I came in." He shot her the sexiest smile. "I was hopeful."

Everything about him charmed her. "What about lucky? Do you feel lucky?"

As he ripped open the packet, she slid the elastic band of his briefs down. Rubbed the back of her hand against his erection, touching him until his eyes drifted shut. Then the briefs were off and nothing separated them except her shorts. She kicked them off before he could crawl back up the bed.

When his body slid over hers, the glorious friction had her gasping. Everywhere his body touched hers, something inside her popped to life. With him she felt sexy and free, a little wild and ready to explore.

She took his erection in her hand. Loved the feel of his skin and the warmth of him in her palm. She savored every noise he made, every grunt and every groan. She kept going, pumping her hand until she felt his fingers on her, in her, and her mind went blank. A mass of wild sensations bombarded her.

When he lifted her legs, pushing them farther apart as he moved up her body, she knew it was time to end the anticipation. Everything inside her had tightened and every cell begged for more. She hovered so close and was desperate for him to push her over.

The tip of his erection brushed over her. She didn't know when he got the condom on, but he did. Then he was pushing inside her. Plunging in and pulling out. The rhythm, each move causing her body to clench in anticipation. Something spun up inside her and she tightened her tiny inner muscles as a way of begging for some relief, and a heavy sigh escaped Holt's lips.

The sounds of their lovemaking filled the room. The steady click of the leg of the bed against the floor. The mix of their heavy breathing. Somehow she heard that over the hammering of her heart in her ears.

She'd turned into a bundle of cells and nerves, all begging for release. She called out his name as he pushed in deeper. When the tightening turned to pulses, she let go. Didn't fight it. Her back came off the bed, and her heels dug in. Control abandoned her as her neck strained and she said his name.

Nothing mattered and nothing could touch her. In that moment she was his and when her vision blanked out she let it be true. The strong arms, the warmth of his skin. She fell into it all as the thumping pulses racked her body.

When she finally came down again, she felt him stiffen. His shoulders froze and his hand slipped underneath her to her lower back. He held her tight against him as his body bucked.

They had been loud and sweaty, sexy and full of need. Now in the aftermath, they lay unmoving with her shouldering most of his weight. Not that she minded. The brush of his skin against hers felt better than anything she could imagine.

After a few minutes of quiet he pushed up on his elbows. "You okay?"

She tried to remember if she'd ever felt this good. "Except for the part where my muscles feel like mush and I can't move."

"Is that good?"

She skimmed her fingers over his shoulder. "Great, actually."

"Nice." He lifted his weight off her and moved to the side, taking her with him. "I'll take great as an answer."

Part of her wanted to ask what this meant, if anything. The rest wanted to savor the moment. She put a hand on his chest and snuggled into his side. In this relaxed state exhaustion overtook her.

She expected to drift off to sleep, but one question kept ringing in her head. "Is it always like this for you?"

"This is a first."

That woke her up. "Which part?"

"I don't sleep with women on my assignments. Ever. I'm not that type." She pushed up and looked down at him. Before she could say anything he started talking again. "You don't believe me."

"I was actually asking about the violence, but it's good to know I'm not a number." Something inside her stomach spun and danced at the idea of meaning more to him than a onetime thing.

"You are not a number. Consider that a guarantee."

She wanted to ask what she was to him, but she feared the answer and went with something safer. "Do you ever get scared?"

"There is fear on every job. The key is in controlling it." His fingers slipped through her hair. "Funneling that energy into something positive that will get the job done."

"The pounding in my head that started with the first attack still hasn't gone away." She'd had a constant migraine since everything started happening.

He rubbed a thumb over her temples. "Stress."

"You get that, too, I guess?"

"Stress? Yeah." He laughed. "I learned to deal with that early. My dad was a hard guy, career military. Nothing was ever good enough. He met my mom in Hawaii and set down the rules about what he expected and the perfection he demanded from day one."

She tried to imagine Holt growing up in that. It explained the stubbornness, the born leader type. "Sounds like a tough guy."

"Others had it much worse." He swept the hair back off her face. "You did."

"It's not a contest." And if it was, she didn't really want to win it.

"But it's a shot of perspective." He shrugged. "He made it clear he loved the military more than us. That we came second."

"You're not him." For some reason she needed to say that.

"I'd rather talk about you." His hand snaked down her back, then went lower.

"For the record, what you're doing there with your fingers is not really talking." When his hand cupped her butt she almost jumped. "But you should keep doing it."

"Does that mean I can stay in here tonight?"

She was prepared to offer him much more than that, but she knew he was a loner. He didn't have serious female relationships. So now was not the time. "For as long as you're in town, you should plan to be right here."

"Deal."

Chapter Thirteen

The news hit the local paper the next morning. The facts were thin, but the story linked Grant's death to that of a brother and sister in a town a few hours away. A separate story on another page talked about a New Foundations member gone missing and believed drowned in a nearby lake. There wasn't a photo or any information, but Holt tagged the story, sure this explained the missing dead attacker outside the Noonans' home.

The paper failed to mention Kelly Noonan was actually alive, which was a good thing, since Connor made sure everyone thought she was dead. She'd been relocated and would soon be given a new identity. Her time in New Foundations would fade into memory, or so everyone at Corcoran hoped. Her time at the camp would only become general knowledge if she chose it, but she was in no condition to make any decision. Cam described her grief as profound.

Holt couldn't imagine what he'd do if something happened to his sister. Rip down buildings with his bare hands. Lose it completely. He would not accept being shipped off and handled, but then he'd be the type to seek revenge. The nasty type.

The people behind the story ached in very real ways, but the fact that a story existed wreaked havoc with the assignment. This was the kind of story sure to whip people into a frenzy. Get them panicked and create vigilantes. Especially the reference to Lindsey.

The story suggested she'd been questioned. The headline didn't blare final thoughts about her guilt, but there were enough dots to make a connection. She knew all three people. One died on her property and she discovered the other two. Pieces of her past, when pulled apart, appeared murky.

The story bore the faint touch of someone trying to smear her name. Careful and cautious, but the intended consequences weren't hard to guess.

Holt slowly lowered the newspaper to the kitchen table with shaking hands. He wanted to shred the thing. Hide the evidence and make sure Lindsey never saw it. She didn't need the hassle. Not on top of all she'd seen the past few days.

But reality stole that choice from him. She

lived in this town. She served coffee to the residents. She chatted with them, lived among them. The gossip would ping from house to house until going anywhere would become difficult for her. She'd be "that" woman. The one people assumed did something wrong even if they couldn't pinpoint a logical reason why.

Holt wiped a hand through his hair. He tried to think of the right thing to say to encompass his fury and frustration, but nothing came to him.

The coffee cup thudded against the table as Shane put it down and leaned in. "I told you it was bad."

He had texted that he had news. He forgot to mention that this bordered on the apocalyptic type. "You undersold it."

"I figured reading it would be bad enough without me broadcasting the details from the car."

Holt wasn't so sure. A warning might have helped him prepare Lindsey. But that was just one regret he harbored. "I shouldn't have called in Carver to the Noonans."

Shane shook his head. "You needed to so we could have Kelly officially and publicly declared dead. Just as important, you needed to send a message to Simon Falls so that we could bring this showdown between him and Lindsey closer to happening."

She picked that minute to walk into the room from the small hallway. "Good morning." Her smile fell as she looked from one man to the other. "What's wrong?"

"Why do you assume something is?" Other than the fact a new crisis did seem to pop up every two seconds. Holt had been stomping out fires since the moment he arrived.

"Your expression, both of you." She turned on Holt. "The fact you just answered a question with a question, which seems like a stall tactic."

The woman did know how to read him. Holt didn't know if that was good or bad, but he knew he couldn't put this off. He shoved the newspaper in her general direction. "Here."

Shane shook his head. "You could warn her first."

"She can take it." Man, he hoped he was right about that. Holt had come to assume she could take anything. She listened to bad news and lived through attacks without so much as blinking. He had to hope this didn't derail her.

She scanned the page, then flipped to read the photo caption below the fold. The whole exercise took about two minutes. She glanced up with a stark look in her eyes. "I am being set up."

And she understood the facts without having them spelled out to her. That made Holt's job easier, but the reality didn't change. Her life and all she knew were about to be turned upside down. "No question."

"I warned you," Shane said.

"Who would feed this information to the paper?" She crumpled the page in her hand as she waved it around.

"Someone at the camp, likely Simon Falls. Not on his own but through someone, so he had cover." The news might implicate others, but Holt knew the intel could be traced back to Simon. He'd keep his hands clean and his name away from the story, but he'd pulled the strings. People had been planting stories this way forever.

"It's rubbish." She threw the paper down and stalked around the table and headed for the cabinets. "Certainly people will know that."

Shane shot Holt a quick look of concern before answering, "People can be fickle in cases like this."

She turned around with an empty mug in her hands. Held it like a shield in front of her. "What exactly does that mean?"

Shane winced. "Expect the town to turn on you."

She had to know that was coming. She might not have been raised in the usual way, but small towns had an energy to them. When news spread, it raced around, hitting everyone and then circling back again with new details.

In a place as tiny as Justice, a story like this could feed the gossip mill for weeks. And as more details emerged, and Holt feared they would, the days would get longer and harder for her.

He wanted to spare her. To make things easier, but she deserved the truth. "We think he's trying to make it difficult for you to live and operate here."

Her fingers clenched around the sides of the mug. "Fine, I'll move a few towns away and do my work."

That might solve some of the immediate social pressure, but she still ignored the bigger picture. "Even without the law enforcement issues, which are very real but can be guided somewhat by Corcoran, I think it's deeper than that. Simon wants you to come to him."

She made a face as if she'd tasted something sour. "Why?"

"To stop you. To confront you." Those were only some of the angles. Holt could think of others. Worse ones. "I have no idea, but this is all too planned. It has the feel of him laying out bread crumbs and waiting for you to follow."

Shane snorted. "Only in this case the bread crumbs are dead bodies."

The comment brought the conversation to a slamming halt. Lindsey looked from Shane to Holt. "Is it wrong that part of me wants you guys to shoot this Simon Falls in the head and be done with this?"

Holt shook his head. "No."

"Not at all," Shane said at the same time.

Her grip on the mug eased and she set it down on the table. "That's why I like you two."

Some of the tension had left her voice, and her mouth no longer fell into a flat line. Holt hoped that meant they were moving in the right direction. Maybe flirting could push her the rest of the way. "Is that the only reason?"

"If so, that's kind of sad for you," Shane mumbled under his breath.

"That's enough of that discussion." She opened her mouth to say something else, but the ringing stopped her. With a sigh she reached for her cell. "The phone. And it's work. Why do I think this is bad news?"

Because she was smart. It was one of the many things Holt liked about her. "This could be the start of a series of nasty calls. Be prepared."

"Let's see." She pushed the button and said hello.

The rest of the conversation consisted of her listening and frowning. She tried to break in a few times but seemed to get cut off. She ended with a "fine" and hung up. "Well, it was nasty all right. I just got fired."

"It's as if Simon has the bad guy handbook and is working his way through it," Shane said. "Of course, he skipped ahead with the whole multiple murders thing."

Holt watched, waiting to see if she would fold or at least scream. She'd earned the right to do so. When she just stood there gnawing on her lip, he asked the one question he hated but had to know the response to. "Any word from Roger?"

"None." She exhaled as she dropped down into the chair next to Holt. "What do we do now?"

He liked her spunk. She didn't suggest hiding or running. She wanted to dig in. All good thoughts, but Holt wanted her here, with a witness at all times, and no trouble. If someone was trying to set her up, giving him more opportunities to do so wasn't the answer.

He had another plan. One that might force Simon's hand. "You? Nothing. I'll take a shot."

Shane frowned. "At what?"

"Who. Maybe it's time I see if I can be of greater service to Simon." The guy hired him and had just given him the "guy" talk. Time to speed up the process and offer him more help than he expected.

"You can do that without breaking cover?" she asked.

Holt smiled at that. "Have some faith in my skills."

"Don't blame her," Shane said. "I was going to ask the same thing."

That one Holt ignored. "Give me a day and I'll handle it."

"How exactly?" She sounded wary as she asked, and her expression looked even more so.

The idea had hit Holt as soon as he saw the paper. Simon wanted to ratchet up the stakes. Then Holt would, as well. "I'm thinking a pretend breakup may be just the thing for our made-up relationship."

For a second no one said anything, and then the anxiety that had been pulsing off Lindsey disappeared. She didn't smile, but she did look amused.

"That makes me pretend sad," she said in a fake crying voice.

"Not half as sad as I am that you won't be serving me coffee anymore." Losing the opportunity to watch her walk around and see that bright welcoming grin made Holt want to kick Simon's butt even harder.

She wiggled her eyebrows at him. "I'm happy to make it for you here every morning."

"And serve it in bed?"

Shane shoved away from the table. His chair legs screeched across the floor as he stood up. "I'm clearly the only sane one left."

"Where?" she asked, clearly confused by Shane's abrupt change in conversation.

"On the Corcoran Team." Shane glared at Holt. "The rest of you lack self-control."

She frowned at Shane. "What does that mean?"

No way was Holt letting Shane answer that one. "Never mind."

SIMON GAVE THE approval for Deputy Carver to be brought to his office. He'd shown up at the gate, fighting angry and demanding access. Normally Simon would ignore the outburst and send Frank Jr. away as a lesson. Simon was tempted to do that, but he did need to talk with the younger man and the time may as well be now.

After the knock on the door and being welcomed in, Todd gestured for the deputy to step into the office. He did more than that. He walked right up to the other side of Simon's desk and stood there. Hovering.

Frank Jr.'s face turned red and he started pointing. "You interfered with my investigation. First, you blocked access so I couldn't ask about Grant. Now the story that raises suspicions about Lindsey. Why?"

The more frantic the deputy got, the more

calm Simon became. This man he could handle, but he needed a lesson in discipline first. "As you can see, I'm working."

The deputy put his hands on his hips. "I don't think you understand how serious this is."

That fast, Simon reached his limit of tolerance. He gestured for Todd to step forward. "No, Frank. You are the one who's confused."

Without saying a word, Todd put the deputy in a chokehold. The position allowed him to take the deputy's gun and radio. He grabbed a few more things. Simon didn't pay attention. He didn't care. The point was to humiliate the man. Show him he was no longer in charge and never had been.

"How dare—" His words cut off when Todd aimed a gun at his head. "What are you doing?"

"Todd will hold your weapon and other items for you while we talk."

The deputy tried to look around, but Todd's gun was right there and his hulking figure loomed over the deputy's much smaller one. He froze and his gaze shot to Simon. "What's going on?"

"We're clarifying the ground rules." Simon closed the file in front of him and folded his hands on top of it. "They've actually been in place this entire time, but you've been running around as if you have a say in anything that goes on in Justice. For the record, you do not."

Never did. Never would. Simon had seen to that with years of laying groundwork, of gathering the right evidence, of building contacts. He ran guns and weapons and whatever else militia groups needed. He supplied and planted the seeds to spread discontent. He caused the battles, then supplied the weapons to fight them.

It was quite a lucrative business, and a place like New Foundations, with the endless supply of bodies and shooters, had proven to be the perfect place to launch the operation. The freeloaders and communal types were long gone. He'd rushed the last ones out and taken care of the ones who refused to go. The leftovers were believers and he was their leader.

"You think you run the town?" The deputy spit out the words in what looked like a last bit of adrenaline-fueled strength. "Half the people don't know who you are and the other half think you're a cult leader."

Now that he had his say, wrong as it was, Simon would have his. "I am the person who gets things done. To do that I make deals, like the one I've had with your father for years."

"What are you talking about?"

Amazing what a well-placed bit of factual history could do to suck the life out of a man.

Simon could actually see the deputy deflate as his shoulders fell. "Your father has been a very helpful silent partner in this venture. He understands that sometimes you need to look outside the law to get things done."

"That's not true."

Simon had no trouble lying, but he wasn't this time. The senior Frank Carver was very much involved with the New Foundations operation. The real business, not the retreat. He'd financially benefitted over the years. And a few times when he needed evidence planted or someone to go away, Frank handled that, as well.

It was a mutually advantageous arrangement, one that would have gone on had the sheriff not gotten sick. With a bit of a leadership vacuum, Simon stepped in on his own. But the Carver family's responsibilities to the partnership had not ended. "With him sidelined, his partnership duties fall to you. I told him to tell you. Since it's obvious he has not done so yet, I am."

"I don't know what you're talking about."

Of course he didn't. One of the things that made Frank Sr. such a great partner was his ability to hold a secret. His life walking on the dark side appeared to be one of them. Until now.

But Simon had bigger concerns than an ill man working his way through rehab. "It's time for Lindsey Pike to meet with me."

The deputy's eyes were wide and wild with confusion. "Then ask her."

"She won't come on her own. She needs an… incentive." Killing Hank in front of her might do it, but Simon wanted to keep that man around for a while. Test him out. See if he was a better choice than Todd as an assistant.

The deputy moved and Todd grabbed his arm, holding him in place. Frank Jr. swallowed as he got the words out. "What do you plan to do to her?"

"Reason with her." And by that Simon meant make her remember.

"About?" The confusion was obvious in the younger man's voice.

"Not your concern." This was between him and Lindsey. No one else. She had set the terms for the battle. She just didn't know it yet.

The deputy's eyes narrowed. "And if she won't listen?"

Simon's patience for the deputy and his questions expired.

"She'll have something in common with poor Grant." When Frank Jr. flinched and looked ready to bolt, Simon held up his hand. "Nuh-uh. Stay still."

The deputy's chest rose and fell on hard breaths. "Why would I help you?"

That was simple. Simon would not give him

a choice. "Because your family is in this. I have taken special care to make sure all the paperwork about the weapons leads back to your father, and by connection, you."

"Weapons." The deputy repeated the word two more times.

Todd laughed. "You are behind, aren't you?"

"You're insane." The deputy tried to look around, but Todd held him in place. "Both of you."

"Determined." Since he was done with this conversation and this man, Simon stood up. "Now you'll go with Todd here and fetch Ms. Pike."

"I won't do it."

And Simon would not play this game. "Then you will die where you stand. You have ten seconds to decide."

Because he had new prey to play with, and one way or another she would be here soon.

Chapter Fourteen

Lindsey stepped out onto the porch a few hours later. She needed a rest from the questions and the tactics-and-strategy discussion between Shane and Holt. If she heard one more scenario where Simon tried to hold Holt and how he could break free, her head would explode.

She promised not to stray, which seemed ridiculous, as this was her house and her property. But she still couldn't look in the direction of the lake thanks to Grant's body being found there. It might take a lifetime for her to feel comfortable again, and she'd never felt fully at ease to begin with.

The right answer could be to sell and find another small town nearby. It made sense, but she couldn't take on one more thing at the moment.

She walked down the back porch steps and toward the small garden. Some of her vegetables were ready to be picked, and shocks of color from the flowers she planted not too long ago gave the backyard a homey glow. She bent down to touch a purple petal. One would never know so much death and danger lurked nearby.

As she thought it she heard footsteps off to her left, through the trees. She lifted her head, ready to tell Holt he could spare the lecture about how she needed to stay aware of her surroundings. Deputy Carver walked into view.

Instead of his usual cocky smile, hiding a heap of inexperience, he stared at her. His eyes were flat and his color seemed off. He almost looked a chalky gray. She thought about asking if he was okay, but she didn't want to say anything that might make him feel welcome, since he was not.

"What are you doing here?" If he'd come to arrest her she just might pass out.

She'd been through so much lately and had handled it all. She was strong and smart by nature, but having Holt as backup increased her confidence. Together, they could beat whatever Simon Falls threw at them.

"I need to take you in for questioning."

Fine, she'd grab Holt and Shane and drag them with her. Let the police or the sheriff or even the FBI deal with those two. But first she had a question of her own. "Are you the one who planted the false story in the news?"

"Lindsey, don't make this difficult."

He didn't deny it. That meant he was in on it and no way was she going anywhere with him without backup. "I want Hank with me."

She took a step toward the cottage and started to call out for help. A hand clamped over her mouth and a strong arm pulled her back until she slammed against a hard chest. A flash of a gun registered in her peripheral vision.

"Do not scream or you die right here." The familiar voice, all threats and rasp and anger, whispered into her ear.

The deputy took a quick look in the direction of her house. "I have this handled."

"One sound and her boyfriend will come running. You do not want to face him in a battle. Trust me." Todd put his face close to hers. "Behave or I shoot the first man who walks out of that house, and I shoot to kill."

She nodded and the tight grip pressing bruises into her cheeks eased. She didn't expect much from Todd and men like Todd, but Frank Jr. should be different. "You're working with him?"

Todd hadn't bound her hands and she used them now. She put a hand on Todd's restraining forearm. With the other, she slipped her phone out of her pocket. If there was a panic button of some type on there, she didn't know about it. She counted on her other skills. She couldn't see to call, but she knew where the text button was and typed all the time on that without looking. This message would be for Holt.

Todd answered her question. "Law enforcement in this county answers to us, and Mr. Falls would like to see you."

The name sent an icy chill running through her. "Tell him to go to—"

The deputy held up both hands as he threw her a wild look. "Lindsey, stop."

She could match his panic with some of her own. But she could also fight, so she hit the last button, hoping she came close to making sense. "He will kill me. You get that, right? You are setting me up to die."

"I know." Frank Jr. reached for his gun.

Todd proved faster. His grip eased as he leaned forward. A knife appeared out of nowhere and the blade stabbed into the deputy.

Lindsey was about to run, to scream, but the sight in front of her riveted her to the spot. Frank Jr. sank to his knees as his hands clutched his stomach. Blood seeped through his fingers. He opened his mouth, but no sound came out, which meant the screaming she heard was echoing inside her head.

Before her muscles unlocked, Todd was on her again. He had her in a strangle hold with the gun right there. "You are a hard woman to get alone."

The menacing words sliced across her senses.

She had to focus to stay coherent while terror ran rampant inside her.

"Holt...he will find you." She stumbled over the pronoun and hoped she saved herself in time.

"Do you mean Hank?" Todd clutched his arm tighter across her neck. "I hope so, since I owe him some pain from those fighting moves in your house a few days ago."

She grabbed for his arm as he choked off her breath. "You admit you broke in and attacked me?"

"Imagine what I plan to do to you next."

Sick laughter filled her ear. Just before everything went dark, she hit Send and dropped the phone.

HOLT WALKED BACK into the family room from the bathroom to find Shane sprawled on the couch. Legs up on the cushions and a stack of papers in his hand. Now that they knew about Lindsey's side business, she'd opened up her office, and with Joel's computer help at increasing her security, they had an easier line to Connor and the office.

The information flowed back and forth, as did Connor's warnings. He didn't like what he was finding on Simon Falls, which was nothing. The photos that Cam took showed large stores of weapons.

Other people might miss the signs; Connor didn't. He recognized boxes and specific weapon types. Grenade launchers and a surface-to-air missile. That was the truly scary one. All of that corroborated what Holt had seen up there.

This Simon Falls, whoever he was, had access to serious firepower. He could cause a lot of damage. If he was a true believer or someone bent on revenge, he likely would. Holt had to hope he was the militia no-government type, not looking for trouble, and not someone seriously delusional or looking to make a name for himself.

But then, Holt had never been the luckiest guy. He wondered if meeting Lindsey had changed all that. Danger and women did not mix. He'd seen his friends turned around and shoved deeper into risk over the decisions they'd made in the name of love.

After spending his entire life honing his skills, Holt couldn't imagine abandoning them for anyone. Of course, Lindsey wasn't just anyone. In a short period of time she'd turned into someone who mattered and he just didn't know how to process that potential vulnerability.

He'd learned the hard way not to trust. A person Holt thought was his friend picked dealing drugs in Afghanistan over him. Shot and left him for dead. But Holt instinctively knew

Lindsey would never make that deal. She'd stand up beside him.

It was the same certainty that helped him learn to trust the team, that kept him so close to Shane and Makena. Now he had to figure out if he had room in that circle for Lindsey...if she even wanted to be included.

Shane waved a piece of paper in the air. "We got the intel back on Lindsey and her past. There's not much under that name, but Joel managed to pull a lot from the fingerprints I scanned and sent."

"What?" Holt looked around for her. Glanced out the window and saw her headed for the flower bed. He'd give her five minutes before he went out there and dragged her back in. During that time he'd watch...once he figured out what Shane was saying.

Shane's sneakers hit the floor as he sat up. "You ordered that we do a full background check on her to be safe."

"I actually didn't." Holt specifically hadn't wanted to go down that road.

"Right." Shane shot him a side eye. "Maybe that was me trying to protect your butt."

Holt remembered the discussion and meant to circle back and stop Joel's digging. He'd even told Connor to put the brakes on. Looked as though the word never got back or Connor purposely ignored the request.

In their shoes Holt would have done the same thing—charged ahead. But that wasn't really the point.

Shane continued to hold up one piece of paper. "Did you get the part where it says Lindsey Pike isn't her real name?"

With one last look in Lindsey's direction and a second of watching her pick flowers or whatever she was doing out there, Holt went to the couch. "I knew that."

Shane's arms fell against his thighs. "Were you planning on sharing?"

"She was raised at the camp, escaped and took on a new identity." Holt glanced at the file and the photo in the abducted child report. A sunny girl with a big smile and missing tooth stared back at him. He saw the intelligence in her eyes but did think the glasses were a nice touch. "And look, apparently."

Shane cleared his throat. "You seem happy with the current version. Can't blame you. The woman is fine, and I mean that in an entirely clinical don't-punch-me kind of way."

An understatement on the looks. The fresh-faced attractiveness appealed to him. So did the smokin' body and smart mouth. If Holt was being truthful, everything worked for him except for maybe the stubbornness, and even that had its moments.

But there was more to it than that. He thought about her all the time, watched her when she was puttering around the house and even enjoyed her off-key humming. He'd never gotten this attached, this sucked in. Never dreamed he could feel secure and messed-up and vulnerable all at the same time over a woman.

So he went with the most natural response to his best friend's prying. "Shut up."

Holt didn't have much else, because he didn't seem capable of fighting this. Whenever he thought about finishing up the assignment and moving on, a tightness filled his chest. The idea of her dating someone else, sleeping with someone else, hit him like a sucker punch to the gut.

Forget the sensation of being dragged under. He was falling for this woman. At rapid speed and without a safety net. He thought back to how he made fun of Joel and Cam—all of them—and now he got it. This one woman walked into your world and everything else stopped. It was downright annoying.

Shane leaned back against the couch cushions. "You know that's your go-to response when I give you grief about being with her, right?"

Knew and planned it that way. "Your point?"

"It's lame."

Holt really couldn't argue with that, so he tried to turn the conversation. "So are your attempts to tick me off."

"We're taking bets, you know." Shane leaned over the coffee table and shuffled through a pile of papers.

Holt was so busy watching the photos and lines of writing flip by that he almost missed the comment. "What?"

"About how long it will be before you're on your knees, begging Lindsey to forgive you." Shane smiled as he said it, clearly enjoying this moment too much.

"For what?" Holt didn't doubt it, but he did want a heads-up if Shane knew something he didn't.

"Oh, there will be something." Shane separated the documents into stacks, using some system in his head.

One page grabbed Holt's attention. He put out a hand to stop others from burying it lower in the pile. "Hold up."

"What?" Shane brought the paper up to the top. "That's Walt Freeland, Lindsey's uncle. He died in a shoot-out with ATF."

Holt picked up the papers as wave after wave of anxiety washed over him. The photo was old, but the resemblance was unmistakable. The jawline. The mouth. The dark evil in the eyes. One thing was for certain—her uncle was not dead. "No, he didn't."

"What do you mean?"

Holt forced his memory to cover and compare every detail. He'd changed his appearance, likely on purpose. Only someone looking would know. Someone who faced the guy every day, or sat across a desk and answered questions.

"Different hair and he's lost a lot of weight, but this guy is definitely not dead."

Shane frowned. "How do you know?"

"He's my boss. Hank's boss." When Shane just stared, Holt tried again. "That's Simon Falls."

"Why didn't she recognize him?"

"She's never seen him in his role as Simon Falls. Few have. I've been up there, trying to figure out how to sneak a photo back to Connor and Joel and haven't been able to." Holt's mind immediately shot to Lindsey. He spun up off the couch and stalked toward the back door with Shane right behind.

Holt's gaze started at the last place he'd seen her and zipped across the yard. He looked for any sign of her as the panic started beating in his head.

"Lindsey?" Shane yelled her name, not being shy about being as loud as he could.

Dread gripped Holt. "Where is she?"

"Look." Shane took off before he explained.

He ran toward the trees to a crumpled form lying in the leaves.

Holt recognized the uniform before he turned the deputy over. Blood pooled around him, and his eyes had gone glassy. He was alive but not for long.

"He's knifed." Holt ignored the ping of his cell in his back pocket letting him know he had a text and stayed focused. He ripped the bottom of his T-shirt and pressed it against the wound. "Where's Lindsey?"

"I'm sorry." The deputy's mouth barely opened.

"Later with that. Where is she?"

Shane scrambled in the grass toward something. He came back and dropped to his knees beside Holt. "Her cell."

Holt unlocked it with the code Lindsey had given him in case of an emergency. As Shane called for an ambulance on his own cell, Holt punched buttons on hers. He found the message without any trouble. Misspelled and almost incoherent, but he knew. Also knew what the text on his phone said. "Todd has her."

As Shane talked in the background the deputy tried to nod as he forced out another string of words. "Took her to Simon...not sure where on the property."

"That's the easy part." Holt thought about the

cell in his pocket and the app that would lead him straight to her. "I'll find her."

They would go and get her. Holt made a personal vow to make it happen and to take out whoever he had to in the process. But right now his entire world focused on the jumbled message filled with typos. He could make out the most important part—"hury, luv u."

Chapter Fifteen

Holt got through the New Foundations front gate without trouble. He expected the guns to come out and Simon to appear. Something that matched the fierce grandness of Lindsey's abduction.

But the camp operated as usual. People carried on, did chores, rode in trucks to the gun range. If anyone knew an innocent woman had been grabbed and dragged up here, they didn't show it. It was possible they didn't care but more likely they didn't know.

The lack of knowledge worked to Holt's advantage. The tracker he had placed inside Lindsey's back jeans pocket, the same tracer he put on her every morning since moving into her house, showed her on the property. But that spread for miles. With Shane's help, Holt had narrowed down a location. An off-limits building on a part of the property used to store equipment.

According to the files Connor had collected,

the place once operated as an employee rec room. Using Cam's aerial photos, they determined that because of the fencing and forest surrounding the area, there was only one easy way into the building. Through the front door.

Trying not to draw attention or pop up on one of the seemingly thousands of video cameras spread around the campus, Holt walked with a sense of calm. His insides had been diced raw, but he didn't let any of that pounding panic show on the outside. Lindsey needed him safe and strong. And she needed him now.

Walking along the lines of cabins closest to the dining hall, Holt passed right in front of the steps to Simon's office. It was the path Holt took every workday, and he did not stray now. Not when anyone could be watching. A quick turn and he slipped between delivery trucks and around a giant storage shed used for nonperishable items.

He had too far to go on foot for the little time he feared he had. Transportation proved tricky. Everyone had to sign out a vehicle to use it. Holt had left his truck in the parking lot per protocol. That left running or improvising. Holt chose lying.

He slipped into the camp's makeshift garage. He had a choice of two vehicles. Both would have GPS trackers and become unusable once he collected Lindsey. That was fine with Holt, since he had other transportation arrangements in mind for the getaway.

With his usual wave to the mechanic, Holt walked right up to the dispatch station. He grabbed the clipboard hanging there on the nail and started filling out the appropriate lines. Holt saw the guy working there almost every day on duty and hoped that counted for something.

The dispatch guy looked up. "I don't have you down for a vehicle today."

"We have some trees down over by the exercise yard." Steady and calm. Holt delivered the line with the dead accuracy of the truth.

The trees were fine, but the story proved easy to sell. The wind knocked things around here all the time. Holt had spent most of his first days cutting fallen branches and clearing paths.

Today he pretended to do the same even as the countdown clock started clanging in his head. He was running out of time and if this dragged on he'd have to turn to Plan B. That consisted of running and finding her and hoping not to get shot as he took off in the most overgrown direction.

Holt handed the clipboard back and waited. He'd know in two seconds if Simon had put out the call to stop him.

The dispatcher didn't miss a beat. He grabbed

an extra set of keys and handed them to Holt. "We need this tomorrow for a supply pickup, so I need it back by the end of the shift."

Holt kept his relieved breath locked inside him. "No problem."

He got two steps toward the truck before the dispatcher called his name. Holt turned nice and slow as he conducted a mental inventory of the weapons he had on him. Last thing he wanted to do was kill this guy or injure any of the members who seemed to want quiet more than a battle.

Any except Todd. That guy had a bullet waiting for him.

The dispatcher pointed toward the sign above the checkout clipboard. "Don't forget to fill the tank."

"Will do." Holt felt the trapped air leave his lungs. He read that faded and peeling sign almost every day. Passed by it and followed the order, which wasn't tough, since there was a filling station not far from the garage.

Not waiting another second, Holt slipped out of the building and slid into the front seat of the truck. With every second he expected guards to swarm and guns to fire. But the big escape plan ran smoothly. No one tried to stop him. No one questioned his right to be in certain areas. He moved with confidence and they responded by giving him room to find what he wanted. In this case, space.

The drive took minutes but lasted an eternity in his head. The building looked worse than he remembered. Rotting wood lined the walls, and the roof tilted as if the whole thing could shift and fall any second. The door had a padlock, but the windows high on the walls of the two-story structure were smashed and broken.

He didn't go right up to the place. He parked and let the engine idle, figuring that might make anyone hiding out here come running.

When the day stayed quiet except for the brush of air over grass and leaves, he turned the engine off. This would not be his choice to hold someone in. In this day with internet videos and all the crime shows on television, the criminals had grown more savvy. This building looked hard to defend and easy to escape from. Just as Holt liked them.

He slipped to the front door and obvious entrance. A quick walk around the place uncovered few other options. Holt decided to go with the door where the ceiling looked the sturdiest.

He thought about what Lindsey's fear level must be, and his temper raged. She sat around here somewhere, alone and afraid. Possibly injured thanks to Todd's manhandling.

Holt vowed he would rip every building apart

and question every person on campus if needed. He had to get her out no matter the cost.

After a quick visual check of the inside through the slim crack in the wall, Holt moved. He pushed on the door and the wood creaked. At least it moved. He could work with that.

Large boxes of equipment, now old and useless thanks to the ever-present Oregon rain, blocked his path. He tried to ease his hand inside. He shoved and worked until he could move his fingers and raise a latch. Breaking in didn't matter to Holt, but this proved quieter and preserved the scene. If his calculations were off or the tracker misfired, Holt didn't want to leave a trail leading back to him.

He used his shoulder to move the door the rest of the way. The hinges squeaked but the door moved. Holt only needed a small space to slip inside. Once he had it, he disappeared into the building.

It took a second for his eyes to adjust to the fading light. The inside was open, with scaling walls and piles of debris in each corner. Dirty windows set up high blocked most of the light and made breaking in or out through them impossible.

The location did not make any sense. No way would Simon keep a valuable asset here. Not with the sorely lacking security.

Holt had walked a few steps before the wrongness of the situation hit him. The quiet bothered him. So did the potential of a tracker malfunction. He was about to turn around or back his way out when he saw the sliver of light. Barely identifiable right there in a small space where the walls supposedly met.

He visually traced the edges. Thought about the layout of the building and the possibility of a room being behind this one. Seemed like an odd choice, but then again nothing should surprise him. He'd been on a wild ride since he got to Oregon. Nothing went as expected and death fell all around him.

Holt went in to investigate. There were boxes stacked and blocking a better look. He lifted everything aside, all while making zero noise. Not an easy task, but he'd do just about anything for Lindsey.

He'd sell his soul for a promise of her safety right now. Anything to keep her from the inevitable confrontation with her uncle. The man who should be dead and if Holt had any say would be soon.

The transformation from sidekick to leader didn't make all that much sense. Usually a big thing had to happen for that sort of change. Holt made a mental note to see if there were any weapon dumps around that time. Somehow, somewhere, this guy caught everyone's attention. If most people never met him, that ruled out charismatic speaker. Very few other alternatives made sense.

Holt slipped his knife out of his pocket to match the gun in his other hand. He'd burst through the wall if he had to. Go in firing as soon as he located Lindsey's position and could account for her safety.

He ran his fingers over the wall, looking for any mechanism to open it. Nothing happened. When he finally ran the tips up and down the outside of the molding around the door, he found it. A small button. He clicked it and heard the grinding of gears. A ticking sound and a thunk and then the door in front of him opened.

Lindsey, behind a thick see-through partition, sitting in a cell that spanned about eight-by-eight. She sat there on the floor with her arms around her knees and her forehead resting on her arms. It took a second to realize she was unhurt. Holt didn't see blood or the signs of pain.

Just as he was about to call to her, her head shot up. She blinked a few times and her mouth dropped open.

That fast, the look of relief on her face turned to horror. She motioned and he started to turn, but it was too late. The unexpected elbow shot nailed him in the back and sent him to his knees.

The next one landed on the side of his head. Something hard and possibly metal. Holt tried to reason it out as he forced his body to keep from keeling over, but the room started to spin and bile ran up the back of his throat.

He forced his eyes open as he watched Lindsey, all panicked and jumpy, put her hand against the partition separating them. Then a blinding pain flashed across his temples and everything went black.

SIMON CLOSED DOWN his computer and removed the hard drive. He had numerous security measures in place. No one but him had computer access at the camp, so unwanted access to the outside world rarely was a problem for him.

He never left anything lying around that he didn't want found. Sometimes that was the best way to spread the word about some bit of news, like the leak about Grant and hints about Lindsey's involvement. Start the gossip and let the members spread it so he could rush in and console. Most times, he had information no one else needed to know.

Today he was in a rush to see Lindsey. She'd been on-site for an hour. Cameras carefully monitored her position. As soon as he had a word with Hank about the new expectations for his position, he would meet his honored guest.

Today was the day.

There was a knock at the door, but before he had a chance to say anything Todd came storming in. "We have a new problem."

Not one to bellyache without reason, Todd was the type of guy who rarely showed nerves and when he did everyone got scared. But he wasn't privy to everything happening at the camp or with the people involved in the activities. More than likely he saw an expected entrance as a problem.

"I see Hank has arrived." Simon had watched it all on the monitors, then sat back and waited to see what Hank would do. He didn't show any signs of nerves or of wanting Lindsey back, which Simon found interesting. "Good. I'm in the mood for a demonstration of loyalty. It's his turn."

"That's just it. He's not Hank."

Something inside Simon crashed. He oversaw every careful plan, every perfectly placed domino. He could ill afford to have Hank be a wild card. "What?"

"Lindsey called him Holt."

More than likely Hank was short for Holt or some other name. They all sounded close, so Simon didn't worry about that. No, he had a much bigger concern and it dealt with ongoing incompetence. "How did they see each other? She is locked up and he is...where?"

Todd didn't hide or back down, despite the rise in Simon's voice at the end. "He is with her. Now. He came on the property and went straight to the barn. Didn't work or go to the lockers."

For Simon to believe that Hank or Holt just knew to go there would amount to a coincidence. Simon didn't believe in those. He would need to be open to those, and he wasn't. Not even a little. "You're certain?"

"He didn't draw any attention. Acted as if he was doing work, but he went out there." Todd shrugged. "You could see the guy's training."

Simon had seen some of that talent on the video screens and believed Hank, or whatever his name was, was checking in just like any other day. But it sounded as if he'd switched to rescue mode and Simon didn't know how Hank would know where Lindsey was or that she needed help in the first place.

He rarely made mistakes but suddenly Simon questioned every piece of information he'd gathered on this Holt or Hank guy. "You followed, I assume."

Todd nodded. "Yes."

"Good work." Now Simon would rip down every wall until he got the truth out of Hank, which raised another issue. "You said Hank went to find Lindsey."

"Found her." Todd's mouth fell into a flat line. "He's locked in with Lindsey."

The cell. One door and a firm see-through bulletproof shield. Just what Simon needed for questioning. "Perfect. They can celebrate seeing each other for the last time."

"Who do you think he really is? I mean, come on. Those skills are impressive. I had the advantage of surprise on my side, but without it..." Todd shook his head. "I don't know."

Simon did. He knew his men could take on one dishonorably discharged military member and come out ahead.

"I'm more concerned that Hank knew about the location of the building. No one goes there." Simon made sure of it. He did some work on the structure, but no one ventured out that far. If they did they were told to stay away.

"It was like she led him there somehow."

"It would appear Hank or Holt or whatever he calls himself has a lot of explaining to do." And some secrets Simon wanted to uncover.

"Are you going to let him talk?" Todd sounded as though he'd prefer the answer to be no.

"Since I can teach him a lesson in the process, of course." One he wouldn't forget because he wouldn't live to talk about it.

Todd's eyes narrowed. "He's a dangerous guy to keep around."

Simon knew that all too well. "But he won't be once we kill him."

Todd actually smiled. "Good."

"And keep watch." This part got trickier. Holt alone was lethal. He could be a true threat if he banded with a friend or a team. "I remember him saying something about having a friend in town. They could be working together."

"If so?"

An easy question. "Lindsey will get to watch them both die."

Chapter Sixteen

She willed him awake.

Lindsey sat on the floor of the cell Todd had thrown her in. With her legs stretched out in front of her, she waited with Holt's head in her lap, stroking his hair as she counted the minutes. He could have a concussion or worse. Could be dying.

The wound bled a lot, but she remembered reading somewhere that head wounds did that and not to panic. Most of the time the skull protected the brain from damage. Still, she used the towel Todd threw in with her to fix Holt up. She worried touching him might make whatever was keeping him unconscious even worse.

This was just one more test in a horrible few days of them. The past hour had been a rollercoaster ride of confusion. The rush of happiness she'd experienced in seeing Holt step up in front of her died when Todd stepped up behind him.

The hit. The way Holt's eyes rolled back into

his head and his body crumpled. The horror show would play in her head forever.

She needed to get out of there and to safety. To check on her people and make sure the rest of her rescues were safe. But first she had to wake Holt up and be satisfied he was okay. In the five minutes since Todd left she'd tried saying Holt's name and singing to him. Kissing his hair and touching his back. Nothing brought him out of his stupor.

She was about to try shaking him when he stirred. He stiffened and then in a snap pushed up to a sitting position beside her. The move came too fast and his head lolled. She thought he might collapse or worse.

"Easy." She put a hand on his thigh and another on the back of his neck. "Are you injured?"

"I'm fine." He started to get up but fell back down hard.

She pulled him closer and leaned his body against hers. "Todd hit you three times in the head."

At least that was what she'd witnessed. There could have been more before Holt ever found her. She had no idea what was happening in the outside world. The small cell worked like an echo chamber, blocking out everything but the fear. That rattled around her until she had to fight off the urge to talk to herself.

"I hate that guy." Holt rubbed his head and hissed. A wince of pain came next.

For a smart guy he kept missing this pretty elementary issue. "My point was, you could have a serious concussion or something else equally awful."

"I'm good." He leaned his head against the wall and exhaled. "I made it seem worse than it was."

"Right. That's why you look ready to drop into a deep sleep."

He turned to look at her without lifting his head from the wall. "Once the first blow came, I knew I was in trouble."

"You're saying you tried to end up in here?" Because that didn't sound smart to her. He should run and get help...shouldn't he?

Yet part of her loved that he didn't leave. He didn't send in helpers. He was the hands-on guy who got things done. Since the wild attraction she felt for him continued to grow and expand, she added being able to count on him to the list of things she liked about him.

He reached over and took her hand in his. "I need to get you out of here."

She was fully on board with that plan, but... "No kidding, but I need you not to pass out."

"I'm not a fainter." He sounded appalled by the idea.

"Can you crawl through glass or whatever that is?" She pointed at the barrier separating them from the outside world. If tough guy wanted to take something apart, he could start with that.

"Cam and Shane are here."

The entire team. For some reason that gave her comfort. His ability to track her so easily should calm her but it didn't feel right. "How did you find me?"

He rubbed his thumb over the back of her hand. "I've been tracking you."

"Excuse me?" She willed her body not to react. Her usual response would have been to start barking questions. She let him come to her.

"It's a tiny dot." He made the symbol with his hand. "Not intrusive."

"I plan to get indignant about that tracking device later. Mostly about you hiding it from me." For some reason the fact that something like that existed made her twitchy.

He shrugged. "It worked."

"And that is why I will thank you. For now." She looked at his face and saw the strain there, tugging at the corners of his eyes and mouth. Every time he moved he let out a small gasp as if his body constantly fought off the pain. Not that he let her see that. No, he tried to bury it. "So, what's the plan? Are we going to sit around and wait to get rescued?"

Holt straightened his back even more. Pressed away from the wall and tried to turn his head side to side.

His eyes slammed shut. "Does that sound like me?"

His stubbornness was going to be the death of both of them. "No, but last I checked you couldn't walk through walls."

"So little faith."

Since they had nothing but time left to wait and see what this Simon Falls creature wanted with them, she kept babbling. "Come on, this has to be the worst situation for you so far."

She expected an agreement. She got a scoff.

He started to shake his head, then stopped. "Not even close."

She looked around at the walls. Air seemed to be pumped in from somewhere, making the spot extra cold, but there were no windows and there was very little hope here. "How is that possible? We're trapped in here, just waiting for our turn to die."

The last part of the sentence ripped out of her. The words scratched against her tongue. She refused to believe this was her day to die, but the evidence kept pointing her to that conclusion.

That was why she wrote and sent that text. She hoped it said what she wanted it to. She didn't throw the word *love* around easily or decorate her mail with little hearts, but there was no question each day she fell a little further in love with him.

"I've been left for dead. That was much worse than this." Using the wall for balance, he slid up until his back was plastered to the wall, and his face went pale. His body seemed to close in, as if the memories proved too much to handle more than in small pieces.

She knew pain when she saw it. The squinting of his eyes and the weight of it pushing on his shoulders. She wanted to rush in and comfort, but she didn't understand his comment. "What are you talking about?"

At first he didn't say anything. His eyes half closed as he stood there. His palms flattened against the wall behind him. She couldn't tell if he was holding his body up or stopping to rest.

Just as she was about to ask, he started talking. His rich, deep voice rang out in the small cell. "In Afghanistan. I figured out a friend, not Shane, was dealing drugs over there. Getting some of our men high at dangerous times. Selling to the locals. Basically, making a lot of money."

He stated the facts in an almost remote voice. As if he'd separated what happened from his real life. She guessed this was a defense mechanism or a way of releasing the poison, but she wanted the thinking and feeling parts of him. Dealing with awful things by using both was the only way to move on.

"I have a feeling I know where this is going." And she feared the story was not going to end with this random guy, whatever his name, remaining one of Holt's lifetime friends. At least she hoped not or she might have to go find him and punch him.

"We were friends, so I gave him a chance to come clean." Holt lifted a hand and pinched the bridge of his nose and then rubbed his eyes. Did the whole uncomfortable guy routine. "I'd missed the drugs and felt responsible. I couldn't help thinking if I'd seen it coming I could have stopped the train."

"I don't think it works that way."

"When confronted with two options—turn yourself in or go home—he picked a third option." Something in Holt's eyes said he was reliving the entire thing as he described it. "He decided to shoot me instead. Left me to bleed out in the desert."

The words shocked her. Everyone read and heard about the horror of war in a distant way. This was personal. A painful memory that appeared to plague him. "How did you survive?"

"I crawled to a hiding place. Kept pressure on

the wound." Holt made a noise akin to a short hum. "It's under my hairline, by the way."

He acted as if everyone possessed his survival skills. As if people got shot at and moved around without help for hours all the time. The idea of him making it out alive made her shake her head in awe.

But none of that compared to the betrayal that lingered in every one of his words. "Your friend actually shot you in the head in order to save himself?"

"Yes, it quickly became clear he was looking for a more permanent solution to my refusal to mind my own business."

"Where is he now?" She hoped locked up somewhere and feeling the weight of his guilt.

"Prison."

Finally some good news after swimming through a sea of bad. "Military, or did he come back and get in trouble?"

"Sort of both but it's military."

"No wonder you don't trust anyone." All the pieces clicked together in her head. The anti-commitment thing. He connected with certain people, likely people he knew before the incident in Afghanistan, but not others.

But now he'd closed his feelings off and buried them down deep. Locked emotions away. Or he claimed to have done so until he'd made love with her. She hadn't seen any signs of him wanting to be somewhere other than her bed that night.

"Do you talk to him?" She couldn't imagine that. Facing down the person who tried to take your life. She didn't even get what the conversation could be unless it included an apology.

"Never. He blames me."

Of course he did. That type would.

"That's ridiculous." Kind of made her want to punch the guy on Holt's behalf.

He gave her eye contact. The type that made it feel as if there was no one else in the state. "And for the record, I trust you."

The words echoed in her brain and she rushed to say the one thing she might not be able to say once Todd got through with them. "Did you get my text?"

"Yes. Very smart."

Yeah, she was not talking strategy here. "I meant—"

"You're awake."

At the sound of Todd's voice, she jumped to her feet. Tried to put her body in front of Holt's, but he held her against his side.

Some of the haze had cleared from his eyes. He still moved half a beat slower than usual and seemed to be holding his head so it did not move much, but the big fierce protector was not far under the surface. She felt him hovering right there, ready to fight.

Todd gestured with his gun for them both to move toward the door. "That's good, since we have a surprise for you."

"What?" Holt asked.

"Apparently it's time to prove yourself." Todd's gaze traveled over both of them. "The boss is ready to see you guys now."

Chapter Seventeen

With each step, some of the fuzz muddling Holt's brain cleared. It still hurt to move too fast or even keep his eyes open for long periods of time, but he was snapping out of it. A few more minutes of rebooting and he would be ready to go.

The point was, he needed to protect Lindsey. Yes, she could handle most situations. But this one was too horrible for her to face, and he didn't want it rolling out in front of her the way he feared it would.

Simon Falls was a psychopath. He'd destroyed people and killed to get to his position. He hid his identity under false names and documents. Lindsey used a cover for safety and to help others. Not this guy. And now he wanted Lindsey. Holt didn't know exactly why, but he guessed it centered on some sick mix of revenge and reunion.

As they walked out of their cell and into the

larger building that contained it, they stayed next to each other into the main room of the old rec center, her fingers brushing his. Knowing it was unwise to hold her hand but desperate to show her how much she meant to him, he touched the back of his against hers. He knew she noticed when she glanced at him out of the corner of her eye.

He spent the rest of the time getting to know his surroundings. He'd been all over the campground. Even got close to the weapons storage. The inside of this place was new. Made him wonder what else he'd missed.

They stopped in the middle of the long rectangular room. Junk and old supplies littered the floor. There was an odd musty smell that suggested the place hadn't been opened in years. The high-tech cell suggested Simon had lots of contacts with the outside world. He clearly did not limit himself to the camp and refuse all worldly possessions, hypocrite that he was.

Todd stood behind them with his gun trained on Lindsey. Smart move. With her in the firing line Holt would not lunge. If it was a matter of him catching a bullet during a fight, fine. But he wouldn't risk her life that way.

So they stood. They waited in silence for what Holt guessed was the big entrance scene from Simon. Holt wanted to lean over and whisper the man's secret to take some sting out of his entry. Holt hadn't gotten the chance to warn her earlier and was about to do so now, but the megalomaniac in question walked in.

He wore casual clothes and had his hair styled so one side swooped over to cover a spot before reaching the other side of his head. He had an assault weapon strapped to his chest and carried a handgun. For a second Holt thought he'd walked into the middle of some stupid coup.

He knew the second Lindsey recognized the man she secretly viewed as her enemy. "It can't be." Her voice trailed off but the surprise lingered.

"Lindsey Pike, or should I call you Beth?"

"Walt?"

He shrugged. "It's Simon now."

Her mouth dropped open and it took a few tries to get it closed again. "You died."

With each shocked sentence Holt felt worse for her. The need to block her from all this struck him hard. He wanted to tuck her away and never let this nutcase or his campground touch her life again.

But he couldn't protect her from this truth. This one walked and talked and threatened. Simon Falls didn't think twice of pulling his niece into his schemes and scaring her for no reason. That made him one dangerous man. And one that Holt would likely need to kill.

"What's the plan here, Walt?" Everything Holt did now was just a stall for time. Shane and Cam had to either fight their way into the camp or wind around and come through the lush greenery and over the huge fence. Since Holt didn't hear gunfire, he assumed they were trying the non-bloodshed method. That meant Holt had more time to waste before reinforcements arrived.

"It sounds as if we all know each other's real names." Simon's smile turned feral. "Isn't that right, Holt? Or should I call you Agent Holt?"

The man was guessing, assuming Holt has a government agent of some sort. This guy did not have the skills to break through Joel's encryptions and multilevel securities and built-in redundancies and fake covers. Holt had faith in all of that…and he wasn't actually an agent. Not in the sense Simon meant.

Simon put a hand behind his ear. "What? No smart reply for that?"

Lindsey took a small step forward. The move put her slightly ahead of Holt. "You want me. Let him go."

Simon shook his head. "That is not going to happen."

"Holt didn't do anything."

That was enough poking. Holt pulled even with her and tugged on the bottom of her shirt again to let her know to keep the other man calm. Fighting and threatening would only ratchet up whatever was wrong with him. He would react and everything would blow up.

"Don't waste your breath. He wants us both, don't you, Walt?" Holt asked.

"Call me Simon. I ceased being Walt years ago after I realized that the weakness gene in our family could be exorcised out."

That sounded crazy to Holt. From the severe frown on Lindsey's face, he assumed she didn't get it either.

"Our family is not weak." And she sounded every bit strong and proud as she said it.

"My brother could not quiet the voices. You run away and then scurry back." Simon shook his head. "I'd like to think this means you missed the discipline and structure of the camp. Have you kept up with your lessons in weaponry? Because that's what we do. Move around and sell them. Provide backup, when needed. It's a very lucrative business. Much more so than yoga, or whatever the hell was happening here before."

Bingo. Exactly what Holt suspected. Not that he cared about being right or the mission with Todd waving a gun around somewhere behind them.

"This is insane." Lindsey hesitated over each

word as if she couldn't believe she had to say them. "How did you even know who I was?"

"Your friend Roger." Simon tilted his head to the side and threw her a sympathetic look. "In the end he was not very loyal, I'm afraid. Pain will do that to a person."

An angry flush covered her cheeks. "What did you do to him?"

"Lindsey." Holt tugged on her shirt again. Her losing her control would hand Simon the victory he craved. No way could she do that.

"He worked for me," Simon said in a voice filled with pride.

Lindsey started to shake her head and didn't stop. "He left."

"And came back. That's the point."

Breath hiccupped out of her. "You're lying."

But Holt feared Simon was telling the truth on that one. Part of Holt always thought the crime scene seemed staged. Then there was the issue with no body. Every other body got dumped right near Lindsey. Why not Roger's?

Holt hated for the betrayal to be true. He knew how deep that sort of pain cut. You wrestled with it for years, turning over every conversation and decision until it slowly drove you insane. It certainly robbed you of normalcy.

"This man betrayed you," Simon said, as if he genuinely needed her to understand. "He came to me with the information about your identity and your secret campaign to steal away my members."

"I thought they were always free to leave," she said.

"That's PR nonsense. People need to stay and be grateful." Simon's careful facade crumpled. "End of story."

"I don't believe you about Roger." She glanced around. "If he's on your payroll, bring him out here. Let him tell me."

"I would, but he is no longer with us." Simon actually smiled as he said it. Looked at Todd and he joined in, too.

The color leached from her face. "You killed him."

"He had an accident, but I can show you his files and the communications going back and forth between us." Simon waved all the words off as soon as he said them. "But we have more pressing issues right now."

Lindsey's body visibly shook. "What?"

"Cleaning up your mess with Holt here."

Holt had expected the threat. Knew it was coming and started the mental countdown to shoving hard against Todd as they wrestled for the gun. Holt had to hope any shot the other man got off would go wide.

This time she did step in front of him. "Do not touch him."

Holt put his hands on her forearms and dragged her back against him. His mouth went to her hair and he whispered, "It's going to be okay."

Like that, some of the tension eased from her body.

"I do believe you've come to care for him. That's a shame, really." Simon spared Holt a glance but not a long one. "He is not who he says he is. I'm digging into that because I want to know who is meddling in my business. I like the idea of making Holt here an example and having him pay a steep price to persuade others not to."

"He is my boyfriend." Her voice rang out loud and clear with that one.

At any other time, Holt would have smiled. Now he had to hold it in and save it for later.

Simon shrugged. "I think we both know you could do better, Beth."

"That's not my name anymore." She exhaled as she stared at her uncle in confusion. "But what happened to you? You were poor and angry. When did you become the leader? Or should I say how? I don't doubt that you eliminated everyone in front of you."

"Beth will always be who you are, just as this place is part of your legacy." Simon skipped over most of her accusations and anger. He went right for one point and stuck there.

"I don't want anything to do with New Foundations."

"Of course you do." Simon used his arm to gesture around him. "I've created this."

Holt wondered if Simon knew he was pointing to a falling-down building in the middle of nowhere as the example for his success. To Holt, Simon's bigger claim was those weapons. He sat on a pile of firepower, which did give him a certain status. Would also make him a target of other people in the business. Holt didn't spare one second of pity for Simon on that score.

"If I end up with this place, I'll turn it into a cat sanctuary or something." She glared at Simon as if she dared him to contradict her.

Simon's mouth fell into a straight line. "I will not dignify that."

Holt thought the idea had potential. "I like it."

The comment earned him a shove from behind by Todd. Holt had almost forgotten about the man and how he hovered. He clearly viewed himself as the second in command to Simon. It was a match made in hell as far as Holt could see.

"I'm going to make you a deal. It's better than I've ever given anyone else."

Lindsey shuddered. She looked ready to heave. "No."

Simon talked right over her. Acted as if she'd never spoken and didn't get to say her mind. "I will allow you to make it up to me for running away and leading your life in ways that do not follow the camp's guidance."

Her frustrated expression mirrored the anger in her voice. "Stop pretending as if I had a choice."

Holt knew the story. The one thing the men in her family had never given her was a chance. They didn't respect her or appreciate her. Holt vowed not to make her suffer from the same thing from him.

"You have a choice now." Simon unclipped one of the guns from his belt and handed it to her.

She stared at his palm and the weapon but didn't take it.

Holt didn't have the patience for this. He jumped in while Lindsey stood there staring in stunned silence. "What is this about?"

Simon's smile grew. "If Lindsey kills you, she gets to live."

Chapter Eighteen

The words echoed in Lindsey's brain. Her uncle, the man she despised and the same one who had scared her so much growing up, actually thought she would choose him. Take money over integrity and happiness.

"Prove to me you are as strong and independent as you claim." Simon continued to push the gun in her general direction.

Holt stared at the gun with an intensity that suggested he thought this whole barbaric exercise was real. Somehow her idiot uncle thought she could be bought and brought back into the sick family fold with the equivalent of a fancy watch.

"It's him or you, Lindsey." Simon's hand stayed steady.

"I won't do it." She couldn't do it. She couldn't kill another human being in cold blood. The heartlessness and sheer depravity of that act tore at her. If he'd offered this deal before to other people, members new and old, that meant others died, and she couldn't think about that.

Beyond all that was one very simple fact. She loved Holt. She didn't know how or why it had happened. It had started out with attraction and she thought it would always simmer there. He'd come into town and eventually move on. Instead, he'd stayed and lured her in.

Even as she'd waited in that cell for death to come, she'd thought about him and the pain subsided. There were so many facets to him. Pieces she kept learning that helped explain the man.

He was stubborn and good, handsome and gruffly charming. He made her knees weak and her head spin. And if she managed to get out of here, she would say it. Somehow.

But no matter what Simon promised or how much he egged her on, she would not capitulate. She would not kill Holt.

That was when it hit her. Not Holt. The choice became so clear then. She would die first.

"This is your last chance." Simon nodded in Holt's direction. "You kill him or I will."

Only if he came through her. "I said no."

"Lindsey, do it." Holt's voice carried over Simon's shouting.

Her gaze flipped to him and she shook her head. Her heart flipped inside out as every cell ached for him. She knew he meant the words.

He'd made her a promise and was willing to ride it into death. The idea of losing him, of living in this world without him, sent a numbness spreading through her. She couldn't feel or taste or think.

But one thing was absolutely clear. She would not be the second person he cared about—and she was pretty sure he did care—to shoot him and leave him to die. No way. He'd survived once. There was no telling if he could survive a second time. And even if he could she couldn't. It would be a move she'd see for the rest of her life.

Shooting him to save her. Never going to happen.

"Be a smart girl and listen to your boyfriend."

Simon was an idiot in every conceivable way. She thought it back then and thought it now. "I'm a woman, not a girl."

"If it's between me and you, you live." Holt's voice, sharp and focused, bounced through the open room and back at her. "I need you to live."

No, no, no. This was not a sacrifice she would allow him to make. "And I want you with me."

"Lindsey, please." The begging in his tone slapped at her.

"I…" She could not make the admission among all this hate. She loved him, but that was between them. Private. "I care about you. I can't lose you."

"You won't."

She didn't know what that meant. Desperation filled her as she tried to ferret out the clues and figure out a safe way through this for both of them. Because her life dragged them to this place. Her vile past. The shocking sight of her uncle. This was all on her.

"You are weak." Simon shook the hand with the gun sitting in it. "Prove to me you understand what's happening here and end this. One bullet to…what do you call him, Holt? To Holt's brain and we restart. All will be forgiven."

Her uncle's sickness spewed out and covered everything. Wallowing in it made her long for a bath. "I don't need your forgiveness."

"Lindsey, be careful," Holt said in a tone she'd heard so many times over the past few days. Not preachy or demanding but concerned.

Simon's face was a mask of pure fury. Red and blotchy with teeth snapping. "Yes, he's right. There is such a thing as respect, and you are not showing any."

He could not possibly think she owed him anything. He and her dad had kidnapped her and stolen her life. The stress killed her mother. That sealed their relationship and guaranteed that the only thing she would ever feel for the man with many names who claimed to be her uncle was hate. "Not for you. Never for you."

"I flipped my world upside down for you."

She listened as he turned it all around and took on the role of savior. She gagged on the thought. "I never asked for it. I was happy with my mom."

"Do not talk to me about that stupid cow."

"Lindsey, no." Holt yelled and reached for her.

She was already moving. She grabbed the gun and pointed it right at Simon's chest. She fired once and then a second time. The gun kept clicking, but it didn't fire any bullets.

Holt blew out a long breath. "It wasn't loaded."

She had no idea how he knew. Her whole body shook as the unspent adrenaline coursed through her. After a few seconds she looked up into her uncle's evil eyes.

"You will pay for that betrayal," he said.

He'd offered her the out and now that she took it he held her accountable. If he wanted to play games, she would. "Now give me one with bullets."

Simon stared at her for long minutes. The hatred pummeled her as the disdain dripped from his lips. When he finally spoke she almost wished he hadn't. "Now it's my turn to fire the gun."

Chapter Nineteen

Holt knew they were officially out of time. Simon had played this out and put Lindsey through the wringer. He planned every minute in order to suck the life out of her. Now she stood there looking devastated with her energy draining into a puddle on the floor.

He got it. She'd been fighting with this man, hiding, for years. In her position, he probably would have taken the shot. But he'd known the gun was empty. It was the reason he didn't tackle the guy and steal the gun. That personality type, narcissistic and unbound by social conventions, Simon thrived on the chaos. He liked to create fear.

He was sick and Holt had no idea how someone as special as Lindsey had come out of a household that included Simon.

"Get on your knees." Simon gave the order as he waved the gun around.

It was a novice move and it worried Holt more than all the threats. "I'll stand."

If Simon wanted to kill him, he could look him in the eye and do it in front of his face. Holt intended to hold firm but then, with a simple nod of his head, Simon issued the one argument Holt could not counteract. Todd stepped up and put the gun right against Lindsey's head.

In other circumstances with family members, Holt might not be so ready to agree one family member would go through with killing another. But Simon's logic had gotten all twisted up. He lived in a place where belief in something should matter, but he seemed utterly devoid of any sort of personal code. His motivation turned out to be simple and timeless—greed.

Holt looked over and saw the fear in Lindsey's eyes and the gun right behind her head, and his knees started to buckle. He would not lose her to pride.

"Very good." Simon turned to Lindsey. "Now you."

She didn't hesitate. She hit her knees, kneeling close enough that their shoulders touched. Her fingers tangled with his. Holt gave in to a second to enjoy the touch. Her hand had turned ice-cold and he took that hesitation to try to warm them.

But he had no plans to die today.

No way was he allowing any harm to come to

her, and this was not his time. He always thought he'd know. When he lay bleeding in that sand, convinced that was the end, his mind had rebelled. Just as he'd accepted his fate, he found a new burst of energy. This was how they would get through this time, too.

He might only have one shot. If Cam and Shane had infiltrated the camp and this building, all would be well. They'd unleash firepower from above and take Simon and Todd right out. There would be others in camp they'd need to interview and possibly remove, but Simon was the key. Take him out of the equation and the whole thing might unravel.

Holt tried to think of a way to clue in Lindsey. They would need to go together. Both duck and roll. Both move and keep going until the shooting stopped. Holt just wished he had a gun. Todd had taken his, but he'd missed the knife. Big mistake.

Simon pointed the gun first at Holt. "You will die for thinking you could infiltrate my camp without consequences." The barrel moved to Lindsey. "You will die for failing me."

"Do it," Todd egged his boss on as he stood over them with a weapon of his own.

Holt gave Lindsey's hand a squeeze as he prepared to go. He started the mental countdown.

Since Simon seemed to be dragging this out

and enjoying every minute, Holt didn't know how much time he really had, so he took one more shot. "All this is over money."

"I am able to do something others failed to do." Simon's ego took over. He shifted focus from the weapon to his perceived brilliance.

Just as Holt had hoped. "You move weapons around. It's not that hard."

"There are causes that need support. A silent partner, of sorts."

Holt had heard this speech from so many men. All of them twisted by the endless race for money. "You don't care about ideals. You're about collecting cash."

"Are you trying to get me to kill you first?" Simon smiled. "No worries. That is the plan. Lindsey should see the man she thinks is so strong and perfect bleed out at her feet. Watch the life drain right out of him."

Holt hit his maximum. There would never be a better time, what with Simon half pontificating and his weapon slightly lowered. Holt gave Lindsey's hand a final squeeze and started moving.

He plowed into Simon's legs as shots rang out over his head. He heard screaming, a woman's voice, as wood and glass splintered above. The room broke into a volley of gunfire and banging sounds.

The dive had Simon falling back and his gun

skittering across the floor. Holt heard thuds and crashes and wanted to look around and check on Lindsey, but all his focus stayed on Simon. She needed him gone. The world needed him gone.

But Simon wasn't the type to go out without a fight. His knee caught Holt in the chin, making his teeth rattle. The older man's legs flailed as he kicked out. Between the punching and shifting, Simon scooted across the floor on his backside with Holt right there chasing him.

When Simon got close to the wall, he flipped over to his hands and knees and crawled, quick and determined like a spider. Holt caught him in the back right before he lunged for the dropped gun. He kicked one of Simon's legs out from under him and leaped onto his back. The move flattened Simon against the floor. He continued to thrash and rear back, but Holt refused to let go. He had his knife out and was about to deliver a slicing cut when shoes appeared in front of them. Boots to be exact.

Simon looked up and Holt followed his gaze. Shane stood there with a gun aimed right at Simon's head.

Shane did not blink as his finger sat on the trigger. "I dare you to keep fighting."

Holt didn't realize he was breathing heavily until he rolled off Simon. The dropped gun wedged under his thigh. His side hit the floor and he conducted a frantic visual search for Lindsey. She sat a few feet away and when he nodded at her, she scrambled to her knees and fell against his chest. With one arm, he pulled her in tight. The other held the knife.

A quick glance around the room showed chaos in every corner. The walls and what little furniture was in there had been torn up and destroyed by gunshots. Todd lay on his back with a small round hole in the middle of his forehead.

Simon survived. That meant he would face charges. Not a perfect ending, but an ending of sorts, which was what Lindsey needed.

And Holt needed her.

Simon was babbling about something. Talking and arguing. Holt ignored it all. He was too busy with the woman in his arms and the thoughts bombarded his brain.

Then it hit him. Where they were and the weapons load nearby, and his brain snapped into action. "We have to get out of here."

He was about to get up when Simon moved. Went from still, as Shane started to slip the zip ties on, to a fighting rage.

Simon came up off the floor yelling. Shane aimed his gun, but he was a beat too late. Holt grabbed Simon's own gun and nailed him in the chest with a bullet. His eyes widened and his breaths came out in a wheeze. It only took a few seconds for him to slide to the floor in a motionless heap.

"This time check his pulse," Cam called out from the other side of the room.

Shane said something back, but Holt missed it. He looked down at the woman in his arms. Her heartbeat thundered so hard he could feel it. A tremble moved through her every few seconds and he knew she'd need some time to work out what had happened today.

"Lindsey?" He wasn't sure what to ask or how to help.

Those wide eyes stared up at him. "Take me home."

Chapter Twenty

Lindsey gasped for breath as Holt pushed into her again. She lay sprawled on her big bed with Holt on top of her, tucked into the V between her legs. It had been this way for hours. They came home, showered and crawled right into bed. They hadn't been out or without each other since.

The bed shook and her fingers curled into the sheets. She tried to regain control of her muscles but couldn't. Her thighs trembled from the force of the pressure against his hips. The way he moved, plunged. He had her grabbing on to his back and not letting go.

She couldn't take another second. She pinched his shoulder to let him know he needed to push her over the edge. No more sensual play. No more making her want him until it choked her.

"Now, Holt." She scraped her fingernails against his lower back to let him know she was serious.

His rhythm stayed steady and he pressed in deep. With each movement he brought her in tight. Held her hips steady so she could feel every inch. But when his fingers dipped below her waist and dragged through her heat, something exploded inside her. Need washed through her as her hips lifted off the mattress.

She exhaled as the tension clamping down inside her released. Her hips moved and her body bucked as the pulses pounded through her. She held on to him through it all. Feeling his body stiffen as the pleasure became too much. The release hit him right as she finished, their bodies in sync until the end.

When she finally came up for air again, she saw daylight outside her window. Birds sang and the rain from the night before lingered in the air, giving everything that fresh scent.

Not that she wanted to be outside. The mix of sheets and his warm body felt so much better. She knew that sooner or later she'd need to get up and face the world. There were questions and documents. The media kept calling. Corcoran Team members called and checked in with Holt to make sure he was okay after his injuries.

That was a lot of reality for her to handle right now. She already had the aftermath of being abducted and stepping so close to death. In her mind, her uncle had been dead for years. Then he was alive. Now he was dead again. She knew she should mourn in some way, but the tears refused to fall.

That wasn't the case for Deputy Frank or Roger. She mentally added both names to the already long list of casualties and felt their losses. And Justice was awash in law enforcement officials. Holt told her ATF, FBI and others had swarmed over the campground. She hoped that meant an end to New Foundations, but only time would tell on that issue.

She rolled over, groaning from all the aches and pains. "I could sleep for a month."

"Do you mean sleep or have sex?" His voice carried an early morning husky grumble. "Because I'll need vitamins if it's the latter."

She kind of doubted that. The man had amazing stamina. Amazing everything.

She threw her arm across his chest and prepared to stay there all day. "We should eat something."

"I'd rather not fly without eating."

The comments had her eyes popping back open. He didn't move, which figured. She sat up and glared at him because he'd earned it.

Finally one of his eyes inched open. He looked startled to see her there hovering. "What?"

"Plane?" Right now she was ticked off at having the information dropped on her like that, but she could easily move through a few more emotions depending on what else he had to say.

He slipped an arm behind his head. "I have to get back for a check-in with Connor and debrief."

"I barely know what any of that means." It all sounded official and work-like. It made sense that he needed to give the information while it was all fresh. She'd had to answer what felt like a thousand questions before she could leave the campground yesterday.

He smiled up at her. "Basically—"

"I don't care."

The smile faded as quickly as it came. "Okay."

He couldn't possibly think she cared about the intricacy of a crime scene and the aftermath. She'd be dealing with her own emotional fallout on this one. Likely for weeks, maybe more. There had been so many shocks and such horror. All that death.

The one bright spot—some days the only one—had been him. He made the terrible bearable. He warmed her heart and set her bed on fire.

She didn't know what kinds of relationships he'd had before. Not serious, from the sound of them. But she knew what this one wasn't—ordinary and forgettable. This transcended. At least it had for her.

But if he could pack up and leave and not

spend two minutes thinking about her, then she had more than aftermath ahead of her. She had a blinding heartbreak that would leave her raw and aching. Just thinking about losing him touched off a pain in her stomach.

She wanted him to just know what to do next, but she needed things spelled out. "Are you coming back?"

He had the nerve to frown at her. "When?"

She sat up, dragging the sheet along with her. "You cannot be this slow."

Wariness fell over him as tension thickened the room. "What are you talking about?"

"There's something between us." It took much for her to admit that out loud. To go out on that limb and hold the risk by herself.

"I agree."

Relief zinged through her. "The question is what we're going to do about it."

Slow and deliberate he sat up. Not the whole way. Just balancing on his elbows as he surveyed her. Studied her as he might a map. "I don't know."

For a second she wasn't sure what question he was answering. The response seemed so vague and so dull. One of those things men said while walking out the door even though they never planned on calling again.

And she couldn't wrap her head around that

at all. They sparked in the bedroom and worked everywhere else. When she gave him a peek into her feelings, he seemed to agree. Now she was getting the "we'll see" type of response.

She had to get out of the bed. An hour ago she would have said she'd stay in those sheets with him for days if he'd just ask. But that was the problem. He never asked. He probably never would.

With the sheet held tight against her breasts, she swung her legs over the side and looked around for a shirt. She snagged his T-shirt and slipped it over her head. Feeling more in control and less ready to be sucker punched, she stood up.

He tugged on the sheet and it fell loose from her body. "Where are you going?"

"Food." That was all she could get out.

Words crammed in her throat and she tried to swallow them back. Part of her knew this reaction wasn't fair. They hadn't made promises or had a deal. She was trying to drag them into something serious, and he didn't do serious. Shane had told her that.

"Wait a second." Holt sat up the whole way this time. "Did I say something?"

"Nothing." That was the point.

"Lindsey."

The pleading in his tone had her spinning

around in the doorway to face him. She thought about saying something clever or making a joke. Anything to ease the tension.

"I've fallen for you." Not at all what she wanted to say. Embarrassment welled inside her, and her stomach did this strange bouncing thing. But she couldn't take it back now. Really didn't want to, because it was true.

He smiled at her, all warm and sexy-like. "I like you, too."

They were not saying the same thing, and the reality of that difference slammed into her like being hit with a bat. Yeah, they were not saying the same thing at all. She was invested and hopeful and looking to the future. He was enjoying the sex. That was what it came down to.

She had no doubt he enjoyed her company. She could see it in his eyes when he looked at her. But the idea of talking about anything bigger seemed to send him running. All the way back to Annapolis this time. She didn't know where it would be next time, but she had no intention of waiting around to find out.

The ball was in his court. Now she needed to make him see it. "I'm going to make you breakfast and then we'll get you packed."

He leaned back against the pillows as if now was the time to get comfortable. "I don't need to leave yet."

His cluelessness actually gave her hope. He wasn't dumping her or giving her the let's-be-friends speech. "Yes, you do."

His eyes narrowed and some of that casual comfortableness eased away. "Why?"

"Because this isn't a hotel." Maybe that hit a little lower than she intended, but it felt good to say that.

This time he climbed out of bed and walked over to stand beside her. "What the hell is that about?"

"You like me."

"Yes." He put his hands on her arms and pulled her in closer.

He clearly missed the part where she had hers folded across her chest. "Fine."

But something got through, because his body switched to high alert and it showed in every muscle. "What's happening here?"

"If you figure out what you feel is more than like—because that's how you feel about a neighbor's cat and not a woman—call me."

"My neighbor has a dog."

He had to be messing with her now. "Fabulous."

"Lindsey, I really don't understand this."

"Right." That was the problem, and for a smart man he was fumbling his way through it. "When you do get it, let me know."

HOLT MADE IT to the private airstrip in record time. He actually got there two hours before their scheduled departure. He had planned to hang around the house, go back to bed. Spend more time with Lindsey.

He didn't want to say goodbye. Didn't even want to leave. He thought things were going fine, and then the questions started. He panicked and then he was in the rental car.

At least they could get moving, since they were all there. Cam was in the process of walking around the plane, performing a safety check. Shane sat on a duffel, using it as a chair as he played with his phone.

Holt did not want to be here. He had no idea what had happened. The day started out so promising. A hot woman and a warm bed. He'd been all over her all night. He knew that wasn't the problem, because a woman didn't beg like that if she lacked interest.

No, the problem came with the talking. Always the talking.

Cam glanced up and stopped working. "Why are you here?"

Holt knew that was a bad sign of the conversations to come. It didn't help that Cam and Shane kept looking at each other, talking some language that they spoke and he didn't seem to.

So he went with the obvious answer. "I lead the team."

"I meant, why aren't you in bed with Lindsey?" Cam asked.

"I would be," Shane said at the same time.

That was just about enough of that. "We need to get home for the debrief."

Holt said it even though he sort of dreaded it this time around. Walking into the apartment meant stepping into a place without her. Her house smelled good, like a mix of her shampoo and something cooking on the stove. He generally ordered takeout when not out on the job.

Man, he really was a confirmed bachelor.

"Wait, does that mean you blew it already?" Shane asked as he stood up and came over to join them on the tarmac.

Cam nodded. "I think so."

Okay, Holt officially hated that conclusion. "No."

Cam leaned against the plane. "Does she think you blew it?"

All of a sudden the guy was a dating expert. Though Holt had to admit he kind of was. He was in a committed relationship. They talked about a future. Holt thought about a future and felt everything inside him clench. Well, it used to. Not lately, but he was sure the sensation of being strangled would come back.

Until then he had a much bigger problem. "I don't know what she wants."

"Oh, boy." Cam dropped his clipboard on the ground.

Again with the looks between Shane and Cam. They glanced and smiled, almost laughed. Holt wasn't loving the byplay. That sort of thing was much more fun when he wasn't the victim. "Okay, enough. What is it?"

Cam shrugged. "You missed a cue. That's almost always it."

Holt didn't even know what those words meant in the context of a woman. "Speak slower."

Shane rolled his eyes. "What did she say she wanted?"

This was downright embarrassing. Holt wasn't accustomed to spilling his guts about a woman. Some things a guy should keep to himself and just handle.

Then he remembered the look on Lindsey's face. A mix of hurt and anger, and he tried to put the ego aside. "I don't know. More time together."

"And what did you say?" Cam asked.

"I like her." He almost shouted the phrase as a plane passed overhead.

They both stared at him and not in a good way.

Cam bit his upper lip. "Wow."

Shane shook his head. "That's terrible."

Tough talk coming from a guy with an awful divorce in his recent past. Holt wanted to point that out, but it seemed like a jerk move, so he let it pass. "Like you would be better."

Shane snorted. "A puppy would do better."

Holt refused to debate based on the animal kingdom. "What do I do?"

"Do you love her?" Cam asked.

The question made him twitchy. Holt got that Cam had figured this relationship stuff out and was happy for him. Holt thought about love and the future and mortgages and felt something inside him go haywire. "It's too soon."

Cam looked at Shane. "I didn't hear a no."

The last thing Holt needed was these two bonding together on this topic. He was just looking for a little advice here. Simple stuff...stuff that he sucked at. "I care about her."

Shane shook his head. "Stop saying that before she kills you."

Holt was two seconds from going out and asking a cat or dog for advice. "You two aren't helping."

"Here's my suggestion." Cam pointed at the bag near Holt's feet. "Take your bag, go back there and tell her what you really feel. Inside. The hard stuff."

That sounded both easy and really hard. Holt

didn't like the downside risk. "Are you messing with me?"

"I'm trying to help you get your woman back before you lose her."

The thought of that knocked out any concern about talking about his feelings. He'd open up all day if it stopped her from giving up on him. Holt hated that idea. "I don't want that."

"Then go tell her." Shane and Cam said it at the same time.

So, they agreed with each other on that one. Holt took that as a good sign.

Chapter Twenty-One

Lindsey sat on her front porch with a glass of lemonade between her palms. The ice cubes chilled her, but she didn't put it down. She couldn't really move. She was too busy sitting and staring and doing nothing.

Getting dressed took a lot of effort. So did the mandatory check-in with all the law enforcement agencies, which she promised she would do. People came by and others called. The newspaper said something about printing a follow-up making it clear she wasn't a suspect. Nice of them, since she wasn't one.

After so much everything, nothing felt good. Well, not really. She couldn't actually feel anything. Watching Holt leave had numbed her inside. She felt hollowed-out and raw. She didn't want to eat and seriously considered burning her mattress. Too many reminders there.

She kept thinking Holt would turn around. Get a mile down the road and realize he'd lost his mind and come back and help put them back together. But no. She didn't wear a watch because then she'd know the exact time he took off, and that was too hard to take on top of everything else.

And this town. She didn't have anything keeping her here now. The people she'd helped could live in the open, free. The memorial services would be set for the others. She didn't know if she could stay in a place made up of so much pain.

She had just decided to take a sip of the lemonade when a truck rattled up her driveway. Not just a truck. *The* truck. His rental truck.

She started to wonder how long she'd been sitting here. By her calculation it had been an hour, but that didn't make sense. Not if he was back. It was what she had wished for but so out of context that she couldn't make the timing work in her head.

The truck stopped and he sat there for a second with the engine on, leaning on the steering wheel and staring at her. She officially had no idea what was happening, and when that tiny bit of hope flickered inside her again, she knew she should tamp it down.

More seconds passed. He must have had the radio on, because at first she heard music but now none.

Finally, after what felt like an eternity, the door opened and he got out. Jeans and a gray T-shirt. Yep, same outfit, so she hadn't lost her mind or a bunch of days. He'd driven to the airport and driven back. Again, not much sense there, but she guessed she'd have to wait and see what he said...if he actually said anything. He wasn't always the best at explaining.

He disappeared again for a second when he leaned across the bench seat. He had something in his hand and he was dragging it. When he came around the front of the truck she got a good look. His duffel bag. The one that had been sitting in her bedroom. The same one he'd packed to leave.

And now it was back. That meant something. It had to.

The hope started doing more than flickering. It danced and bounced. Some of the anger and sadness that had been weighing her down since he'd left lifted. She took a big gulp of lemonade to make sure she wasn't dreaming. The pucker told her she wasn't.

She didn't know when she'd stood up, but she had. She had a glass dangling from her hand and her heart right out there for everyone to see. It was kind of embarrassing how much she loved this man. So few days had passed and yet she felt as if her life had become tied to his.

Without thinking about it or remembering a thing, she met him at the steps to the porch. She wasn't sure what that meant, so she didn't pick at it too much. She stood one above him, which put them face-to-face. She could look into those dark eyes. Wariness lingered there. She sure got that.

It seemed to her that he should be the first to say something. But when his gaze toured her face but he stayed quiet, she jumped in. "What are you doing here?"

"This is where I want to be." He shuffled his weight back and forth. Not really something he did. He never fidgeted. If anything, he could hold still for what felt like hours. It always struck her as a bit freaky, but the wounded puppy look was sure charming.

And that was such a better answer than the ones he'd given her before. It didn't make her want to scream or strangle him. Both good signs. "You said you have to go home. Something about briefings."

She didn't remember all the other stuff. Basically he talked about flying out and her brain shut down. Maryland meant going across the country without her. She hated everything about that plan.

"I should, yeah. But I'd rather be here with you. Anywhere with you." He shrugged. "I mean you can come home with me if you want. So long as we're in the same house and same bed, I'm good."

The responses just kept getting better and better. This one shot off the charts.

Here she sat trying to figure out where and how she fit in. Then in a few words he'd made her an offer. Quick and to the point. He wasn't a guy who lingered over facts and details.

She knew when he put it out there he meant it. She could count on it. And she just might.

But she tried not to get too excited, because he looked more shell-shocked than in love. His skin had an odd dullness to it and he looked as though he should consider sitting down. "Why the change?"

"Cam and Shane basically told me I'm an idiot."

She smiled as she set the glass down on the porch and out of kicking range. After spending a few days with Shane she could almost hear the conversation. "I like them."

"Don't be fooled. They're idiots, too." Holt matched her and dropped his bag. Didn't put it on the ground or near the car. No, he walked up two steps and put it on the porch and then returned to where he was standing below her.

For some reason that struck her as significant. It would be better if he put it in her bedroom or loaded her stuff in his truck to leave. Both worked for her.

She had a home and a life here, but she could shift. She could anchor herself to him. After all these years obsessing over the same thing, it might be good to find a new hobby. Find new work and another passion. Though her passion for him did consume her at the moment.

The warm sun pounded down on them. The temperature had turned and the unseasonably cool weather had moved out, leaving a bright blue sky behind. Summer in Oregon was a beautiful thing. The water close by and the towering trees lining the mountains. Between the fresh air and the good food, she could almost forget all the killing.

Almost.

Neither of them said anything for a minute. She was content to stand there and look at him. The temptation to brush back his hair. All that touching in the bedroom. She wanted that feeling of intimacy no matter where they were together.

The bag and sweet words already told her what she needed to know about his commitment. None of this came easy to him, but he was trying. This was hard for him, but he pushed through and she knew he did it all for her. Maybe because his friends gave him a hard time, but she could accept that.

She was about to take pity on him when he started talking. "When I said I cared for you I meant it."

"I know." But the lukewarm phrase made her back teeth slam together. Instinctively, she knew it was a lot for him to say. That it was a big deal. But she wanted more. After a lifetime of settling and helping others, she was ready to grab something for herself. And she wanted it to be him.

He took one of her hands in both of his. Played with her fingers and caressed her palm. The gentle touches had her nerve endings screaming for more. "I will never lie to you."

"I get that, too."

"I'm going to mess up." He peeked up at her. "A lot. This relationship stuff doesn't come naturally to me, and the strength of my feelings for you scares me. They knock me sideways and that's never happened before."

She loved every word.

"I see you and I want to strip your clothes off." He threw her a lopsided smile. "It was that way from day one. Something very primal and instinctive."

But she wanted this—no, needed this—to be about more than sex. She had already said the words, and she'd stopped short. He needed to make part of the journey now. "Tell me what you really want from me. I know what I want from you, but what are you looking for?"

"Everything."

"Holt…"

"I've had a messed-up life. A weird relationship with my dad and nearly dying." He shrugged. "Those aren't excuses for anything. More like explanations."

"I get it." She did. "The past shapes us. I mean, really. Look at my life and my obsession." So much of who she was and how she reacted to things came from back then. She'd set her entire adult life around a place she professed to hate.

For her, New Foundations and everything that had happened this week were about closure and moving on. For the first time she felt as if she had the power and strength to make it happen.

"Any chance you're looking for a new one?"

She missed the comment, but she caught the smile. It was infectious. When he opened up and let his feelings shine through, he was even more attractive. She loved the brooding side. The darkness and his need to control and protect. Those were all parts of him and together they made up this beautiful, complex, wonderful man.

His comment finally registered. "Wait, what did you say?"

"Obsession. If you're looking for one I'd be happy to volunteer." He started ticking off points on his fingers. "I don't smoke. Not a big drinker except for a beer with football. I can cut firewood and take you to dinner."

The words hit her and that hope turned into a raging bonfire. He stood there handing her everything. Stuff she'd always dreamed of and things she didn't even know she wanted until they came in a package that included him.

She wrapped her arms around his neck. The poor thing looked lost and ready to be sent away. But she wouldn't do that. She hadn't wanted to do it earlier, but the decision to stay had to be his.

But pushing him out. That was not going to happen again. From now on she'd make him stick around and fight. About work and home and friends and even what was for dinner. If they were going to try this, going to make it work, they had to be a partnership, and sometimes that was a rocky thing.

"Are you volunteering for this obsession position?"

He rubbed his hands up and down her back. "Since I'm half in love with you I thought it might be good if you decided you couldn't live without me. You know, be tied to me and not want to let me go."

And there she went. Totally, fully in love with

him. No partway. No think about it. No waiting to see. It was right there in front of her and she grabbed it.

But they had to backtrack a bit. They'd jumped over the simple steps like getting to know each other and spending time together. They could circle back to those. For now, she was fine with the rest moving at top speed. They'd fill in the blanks, from simple things like meeting his sister to the more complicated, like where to live.

He sighed into her hair. "I'm not great at this, but—"

"Wrong. You might be a slow starter, but you're pretty great at it." She kissed his cheek and then his neck. "At so many things. At most things, actually. Come to think of it, you're not going to be easy to live with."

"I already listed the pros."

She gave in to the temptation and ran a hand through his hair. "All very impressive."

"Does this mean I can stay?"

She dropped a quick kiss on his mouth. "Just try to leave me again."

"That's exactly what a man likes to hear." He picked her up and her legs wrapped around his. They stood there in the sunshine with the warmth pouring over them. "The debrief can wait. Let's go check out that bed again. I think

I left a bit too early this morning, but we can fix that."

He was full of great ideas all of a sudden. She didn't know who she should thank, Cam or Shane or both, for the nudge in the right direction, but she would. Because right now she'd never been happier. Never stood on the cusp of getting everything she wanted. And she loved the sensation. "Only if you promise we'll stay in there all day."

He smiled. "Deal."

Chapter Twenty-Two

Cam read the text from Holt. Read it a second time just so he could enjoy it. Looked as though the big man had found the right words to win Lindsey over. Either that or she'd taken pity on him and let him stay. Either way, Holt won.

Lindsey was a good woman. Right for him. Strong and smart, beautiful and able to handle Holt's personality. They fit together. Cam had noticed the sparks right away.

Cam knew how it felt. Since he'd been with Julia, everything felt right. The danger worried him. Not for him but for her. He'd lived his entire life on the edge. He didn't question it, but he'd feared it would drive them apart, but she insisted she went into the relationship knowing about his background and need for danger.

He'd gone from "no, thank you" on commitments to craving one. He even had the ring picked out...not that Julia knew that. Only Joel knew and Connor, since Cam didn't know a thing about rings and Connor was already married.

Technically, it was too early. Not by Cam's standards. He'd known after day four that Julia was the one. But he was willing to wait a respectable amount of time, however much she needed. He just hoped that didn't extend past six months, because a guy could only take so much. When he decided he wanted to see his bride walk down the aisle, he wanted it to happen now.

With Holt partnering up, that left one single guy on the team. Shane wasn't easy to pin down. Well, for others to pin down. The identity of the right woman was not really a mystery. He just had to get out of his own way long enough to give her a chance. Not make such a big deal of the little problems between them. Let go of his past once and for all.

If the rest of them shunned commitment, Shane was openly hostile to it. Divorce would do that to a guy, and his was of the nasty variety.

But people changed. The rest of the team had. One by one they'd paired up. They'd found stability and women and a home to go to. None of them were ever party types. Their jobs didn't allow that, because they had to be packed and ready to go on short notice. Being drunk would be a hindrance to that.

Seven down, one to go. As soon as Cam filled the office in on Holt's chosen vacation destination, the pressure would be on Shane. Good thing the guy could handle it. Could handle anything...except Makena Kingston.

Cam slipped his phone into his back pocket. "It's just the two of us on this ride. Holt decided to wait here for a few days."

A stupid grin split across Shane's face. "A few? I guess that means he's staying or we're going to have to move her to him. Either way you know we'll end up helping, right?"

"Wouldn't you stay if you were him? Pretty woman he's falling for and a warm bed." It was a test and Cam had a feeling Shane was about to fail.

"You're asking the wrong guy. The staying thing is not for me. Not now and not ever. If you don't believe me, ask my divorce lawyer. I'm still paying his bill." Shane loaded the bags into the plane's cargo area. They had their personal items plus a few boxes of intel about the campground. Another few about the weapons.

Cam decided to ignore the divorce because that was too tough to operate around. "You notice you're the only one around here not paired up."

After dropping a few hints about the woman involved in this case and Holt's interest in her, the Annapolis office decided he was taken. They were already talking about Shane being next, and last, and poor Holt was still in the getting-to-know-you phase.

Shane kept loading. Kept his head down. Ignored most of the conversation and stuck to short answers. In other words, the usual.

After a few minutes of quiet he finally piped up. "You've all lost your minds. Never seen guys go from confirmed bachelors to husbands so fast. Half of you are in relationships that are right on the verge of ending with a ring."

Cam couldn't argue. "It's your turn next."

The reply came fast and sharp. "Nope. No to the serious dating and definitely not to anything that will lead to a ring. I've already done that. In fact, I think that means you guys are behind me."

"You never know who you'll meet. Maybe it's someone you already know." But Cam knew about the panic that set in when the others paired off. He'd been there. Breezed through the dating stages with Julia and hit the denial part pretty hard.

But there's that one woman. The one who turns your head and gets you thinking about things you never dreamed about.

Cam had found that with Julia. All the guys now had it. All but Shane.

"Again, I've been married," Shane pointed

out. "I know all about the realities, and you can't sell the institution to me."

Since the topic of Shane's divorce never led to a good conversation, Cam tried to come at this from another direction. "Looks like we'll have a few days off."

"Sounds good to me." Shane loaded the last box and shut the door. "I can't remember the last time I've been home."

The guy walked right into the trap. "Right about the time Shane's sister moved down the road."

Shane's shoulders froze for a second. Then he went back to work. "Yep."

Shane had it bad for Makena. It was one of those attractions you could see. Well, everyone but the two people trying hard not to be in the relationship. Makena denied it. Shane denied it. Holt ignored it. It was an interesting trifecta of dysfunction.

But that didn't change the fact that Shane watched Makena move and eat. They talked in groups and shut down around each other when it was just the two of them. It wasn't always that way...but then Makena had grown up.

"She's still around, right?"

Shane snorted. "You know where Makena is. Stop matchmaking."

Easier said than done when the wives were

involved and poking around. "I was wondering if you did."

"She's off-limits."

"Right." The whole baby sister of Holt thing. Dating the boss's sister was problematic. Adding in the fact that her brother and Shane were best friends just complicated things.

"I'm serious." And Shane growled that out as if to make sure Cam got it. "Don't help me."

"We'll see."

* * * * *

Don't miss the heart-stopping conclusion of HelenKay Dimon's miniseries
CORCORAN TEAM:
BULLETPROOF BACHELORS
*when TAMED goes on sale next month.
Look for it wherever Harlequin Intrigue books and ebooks are sold!*

LARGER-PRINT BOOKS!

HARLEQUIN

Presents

PASSION GUARANTEED SEDUCTION

GET 2 FREE LARGER-PRINT NOVELS PLUS 2 FREE GIFTS!

YES! Please send me 2 FREE LARGER-PRINT Harlequin Presents® novels and my 2 FREE gifts (gifts are worth about $10). After receiving them, if I don't wish to receive any more books, I can return the shipping statement marked "cancel." If I don't cancel, I will receive 6 brand-new novels every month and be billed just $5.30 per book in the U.S. or $5.74 per book in Canada. That's a saving of at least 12% off the cover price! It's quite a bargain! Shipping and handling is just 50¢ per book in the U.S. and 75¢ per book in Canada.* I understand that accepting the 2 free books and gifts places me under no obligation to buy anything. I can always return a shipment and cancel at any time. Even if I never buy another book, the two free books and gifts are mine to keep forever.

176/376 HDN GHVY

Name	(PLEASE PRINT)	
Address		Apt. #
City	State/Prov.	Zip/Postal Code

Signature (if under 18, a parent or guardian must sign)

Mail to the **Reader Service:**
IN U.S.A.: P.O. Box 1867, Buffalo, NY 14240-1867
IN CANADA: P.O. Box 609, Fort Erie, Ontario L2A 5X3

Are you a subscriber to Harlequin Presents® books and want to receive the larger-print edition?
Call 1-800-873-8635 today or visit us at www.ReaderService.com.

* Terms and prices subject to change without notice. Prices do not include applicable taxes. Sales tax applicable in N.Y. Canadian residents will be charged applicable taxes. Offer not valid in Quebec. This offer is limited to one order per household. Not valid for current subscribers to Harlequin Presents Larger-Print books. All orders subject to credit approval. Credit or debit balances in a customer's account(s) may be offset by any other outstanding balance owed by or to the customer. Please allow 4 to 6 weeks for delivery. Offer available while quantities last.

Your Privacy—The Reader Service is committed to protecting your privacy. Our Privacy Policy is available online at www.ReaderService.com or upon request from the Reader Service.

We make a portion of our mailing list available to reputable third parties that offer products we believe may interest you. If you prefer that we not exchange your name with third parties, or if you wish to clarify or modify your communication preferences, please visit us at www.ReaderService.com/consumerschoice or write to us at Reader Service Preference Service, P.O. Box 9062, Buffalo, NY 14240-9062. Include your complete name and address.

HPLP15